M000074100

PENGUIN MODERN CLASSICS
The Cat and Shakespeare

RAJA RAO (1909–2006), a path-breaker of Indian writing in English, was born in Hassan, Mysore. After he graduated from Madras University, he went on to the University of Montpellier in France on a scholarship. He moved to the United States in 1966, where he taught at the University of Texas at Austin until 1983, when he retired as emeritus professor.

A powerful and profound writer, and a superb stylist, Rao successfully and imaginatively appropriated English for the Indian narrative. He was honoured with India's second-highest civilian award, the Padma Vibhushan, in 2007, the Sahitya Akademi Award in 1964, and the Neustadt International Prize for Literature in 1988.

R. PARTHASARATHY is a poet and translator. The author of the long poem 'Rough Passage', he edited the influential anthology *Ten Twentieth-Century Indian Poets*. His translation of the fifth-century Tamil epic, the *Cilappatikāram*, was awarded the 1995 Sahitya Akademi Award. He is a professor emeritus of English and Asian studies at Skidmore College in Saratoga Springs, New York. He was Raja Rao's editor from 1974 to 1998.

RAJA RAO

The Cat and Shakespeare

With an Introduction by R. Parthasarathy

PENGUIN BOOKS

PENGUIN BOOKS
Published by the Penguin Group
Penguin Books India Pvt. Ltd, 7th Floor, Infinity Tower C,
DLF Cyber City, Gurgaon 122 002, Haryana, India
Penguin Group (USA) Inc., 375 Hudson Street, New York,
New York 10014, USA
Penguin Group (Canada), 90 Eglinton Avenue East, Suite 700,
Toronto, Ontario, M4P 2Y3, Canada
Penguin Books Ltd, 80 Strand, London WC2R 0RL, England
Penguin Ireland, 25 St Stephen's Green, Dublin 2, Ireland
(a division of Penguin Books Ltd)
Penguin Group (Australia), 707 Collins Street, Melbourne,
Victoria 3008, Australia
Penguin Group (NZ), 67 Apollo Drive, Rosedale, Auckland 0632,
New Zealand
Penguin Books (South Africa) (Pty) Ltd, Block D, Rosebank Office Park,
181 Jan Smuts Avenue, Parktown North, Johannesburg 2193, South Africa

Penguin Books Ltd, Registered Offices: 80 Strand, London WC2R 0RL,
England

Published by Penguin Books India 2014
Copyright © Susan Raja Rao 2014
Introduction copyright © R. Parthasarathy 2014

Typeset in Goudy Old Style by CyberMedia Services Ltd, Gurgaon
Printed at Replika Press Pvt. Ltd, India

A PENGUIN RANDOM HOUSE COMPANY

The Cat and
Shakespeare

INTRODUCTION

In 1929, a young Brahmin from Hyderabad in southern India set out for France, for Montpellier in fact, 'that ancient Greek and Saracenic town, so close to Sète where Valéry was born,'[1] at the invitation of Sir Patrick Geddes (1854-1932), the Scottish town planner, who had established the Collège des Écossais there. It was, however, at Soissons, where Abelard was imprisoned and condemned, that the Brahmin Raja Rao (1908-2006) wrote his first stories, 'Javni' and 'The Little Gram Shop'. *Kanthapura* was, for the most part, written in a thirteenth-century French castle in the Alps, and published in 1938 by Allen and Unwin.

'Unless you be a pilgrim you will never know yourself.'[2] In his search for a guru, Rao wandered in and out of the ashrams of Pandit

---

1. Raja Rao, *The Policeman and the Rose: Stories*. Delhi: Oxford University Press, 1978, p. xiv.
2. Raja Rao, *The Chessmaster and His Moves*. New Delhi: Vision Books, 1988, p. 1.

Taranath (1891–1942), near Mantralayam on the Tungabhadra River; Sri Aurobindo (1872–1950) in Pondicherry; Ramana Maharshi (1879–1950) in Tiruvannamalai; Narayana Maharaj (1885–1945) in Kedgaon, near Pune; and Mahatma Gandhi (1869–1948) in Sevagram, near Wardha. His search ended in 1943, in Trivandrum, when he met Sri Atmananda (1883–1959).

In 1947, Oxford University Press, Bombay published *The Cow of the Barricades and Other Stories*. Rao's spiritual experiences as a Vedantin form the basis of his next two novels, *The Cat and Shakespeare*—published as 'The Cat' in the Summer 1959 issue of the *Chelsea Review*, New York, and in 1965 by Macmillan—and *The Serpent and the Rope*, published in 1960 by John Murray.

Rao moved to Austin, Texas in 1966 to begin teaching Indian philosophy at the University of Texas, a position he held till his retirement in 1980. In 1978, as his editor at Oxford University Press, Madras, I published *The Policeman and the Rose: Stories*. Meanwhile, in 1965, Rao's fourth novel, *Comrade Kirillov*, had appeared in a French translation in Paris. And, finally, in 1988, exactly fifty years after the publication of his first novel, Vision Books, New Delhi published *The Chessmaster and*

His Moves, the first volume of a trilogy, to be followed by *The Daughter of the Mountain* and *A Myrobalan in the Palm of Your Hand*. The novel was awarded the tenth Neustadt International Prize for Literature in 1988. Vision Books also published *On the Ganga Ghat* in 1993, and *The Meaning of India*, a collection of essays, in 1996.

One of the most innovative novelists of the twentieth century, Rao departed boldly from the European tradition of the novel, which he indigenized in the process of assimilating material from the Indian literary tradition. He put the novel to uses to which it had not perhaps been put before, by exploring the metaphysical basis of writing itself—of, in fact, the word. In the Indian tradition, literature is a way of realizing the Absolute (Brahman) through the mediation of language.

As a writer, Rao's concern is with the human condition rather than with a particular nation or ethnic group. Rao told me one pleasant February morning in 1976 in Adyar, Madras:

> One of the disciplines that has interested me in Indian literature is its sense of *sadhana* (*exercitia spiritualia*)—a form of spiritual growth. In that sense, one is alone in the

world. I can say that all I write is for myself. If I were to live in a forest, I would still go on writing. If I were to live anywhere else, I would still go on writing, because I enjoy the magic of the word. That magic is cultivated mainly by inner silence, one that is cultivated not by associating oneself with society, but often by being away from it. I think I try to belong to the great Indian tradition of the past when literature was considered a *sadhana*. In fact, I wanted to publish my books anonymously because I think they do not belong to me. But my publisher refused.[3]

The house of fiction that Rao has built is thus founded on the metaphysical and linguistic speculations of the Indians. It is to the masters of fiction in our time, such as Proust and Joyce, that we must ultimately turn for a writer of comparable stature.

One of the difficulties a reader encounters in the presence of Indian literature in English is that of understanding the nature of the world projected by the text and, by implication, the strategies of discourse adopted by the writer

---

3. R. Parthasarathy, 'The Future World Is Being Made in America: An Interview with Raja Rao', *Span* (September 1977): 30.

to nativize the English language. Not enough attention has so far been paid to this in the Indian context, with the exception of Braj B. Kachru's study.[4] Kachru examines the problem from the perspective of a sociolinguist. I will try, however, to explore its implications generally in the context of Indian literature in English, and specifically in the context of the fiction of Raja Rao. His fiction offers a paradigm of Indian literature in English with all its contradictions.

The preface to *Kanthapura* is revolutionary in its declaration of independence from English literature, and it has, as a result, become a classic stylistic guide for non-native English writers everywhere.

> There is no village in India, however mean, that has not a rich *sthala-purana*, or legendary history, of its own. Some god or god-like hero has passed by the village . . . the Mahatma himself, on one of his many pilgrimages through the country, might have slept in this hut, the low one, by the village gate. In this way the past mingles with the present, and the gods mingle with men to

---

4. Braj B. Kachru, *The Indianization of English: The English Language in India*. Delhi: Oxford University Press, 1983.

make the repertory of your grandmother always bright. One such story from the contemporary annals of my village I have tried to tell.[5]

Kanthapura is the story of how Gandhi's struggle for independence from the British came to a remote village in southern India. The struggle takes the form, on the one hand, of non-violent resistance to Pax Britannica and, on the other, of a social protest to reform Indian society. References to specific events in India in the late 1920s and early 1930s suggest that the novel has grown out of a distinct historical context. Told by an old woman, Achakka, the story evokes the spirit and discourse of the traditional folk narratives, the puranas. In an attempt to elucidate Rao's intentions, I shall examine the preface as an introduction to his own fiction.

Since the rise of the novel in the eighteenth century, its philosophical bias has been towards the particular; hence, its focus on the individual in an objective world. An entirely opposite view is expressed in *The Serpent and the Rope*: India is

5. Raja Rao, *Kanthapura*. London: Allen and Unwin, 1938. Reprinted 1963, New York: New Directions. Subsequent citations from the American edition are indicated in the text parenthetically by page number.

'perhaps the only nation that throughout history has questioned the existence of the world—of the object'.[6] When a non-native English writer such as Rao chooses this specific genre rather than one that is traditional to his own culture, the epic, for instance, and further chooses to project this genre in a second language, he takes upon himself the burden of synthesizing the projections of both cultures. Out of these circumstances, Rao has forged what I consider a truly exemplary style in Indian literature in English—in fact, in world literature in English. He has, above all, tried to show how the spirit of one culture can be possessed by, and communicated in, another language.

English as a code is now universally shared by both native and non-native speakers. What is not always shared or recognized are the manifestations of a specific culture embedded by the writer in the language. Though the language can now be taken for granted, what cannot any longer be taken for granted are the cultural deposits transmitted by the language. To understand them, the reader, especially if he

---

6. Raja Rao, *The Serpent and the Rope.* London: John Murray, 1960. Subsequent citations from this edition are indicated in the text parenthetically by page number.

is a native speaker, must equip himself with a knowledge of the writer's sociocultural milieu. Would he not be expected to do so if he were to read an English translation of, say, the Mahabharata or, for that matter, the Iliad?

Culture determines literary form, and the form of the novel from cultures within India has been strongly influenced by those cultures themselves, resulting in something different from the form of the novel in the West. Rao himself is of the opinion that an Indian can never write a novel; he can only write a purana. The puranas are sacred history included in the canon of scripture, and they tell the stories of the origin of the universe, the exploits of gods and heroes, and the genealogies of kings. Their impact on the minds and imaginations of the people of India has been profound. Through them the Vedas and the Upanishads and the ideas of the great tradition of Hinduism were communicated by intention and organized effort to the people and woven into their lives in festivals and rituals. The Mahabharata and the Ramayana were expressly composed for the same purpose. There is, at least in southern India, an unbroken tradition of recitation of the two epics by ruler and teacher in the vernacular languages. The epics were recited in the form of stories by the *sutapauranikas*, the bards who recite the puranas.

Sanskrit is, in fact, an obsession with Rao: 'It is the source of our culture . . . and I have wished a thousand times that I had written in Sanskrit.'[7] Intellectually and emotionally, he is deeply rooted in the Indian tradition, especially in the philosophical tradition of the Advaita ('monism') Vedanta of Sankara (eighth century). Sankara was interested in the nature of the relationship of the individual self (atman) with the universal Self (Brahman). He insisted that they were identical (*tat tvam asi*, 'You are That'),[8] and that all appearances of plurality and difference arose from the false interpretation of the data presented by the mind and senses. He therefore rejected subject–object dualism. The only reality is Brahman. For Sankara, liberation (moksha) was the ultimate aim, and he defined it as intuitive knowledge of the identity of atman and Brahman, and not, it is to be remembered, as union with God.

Rao's ideas of language, especially the empowerment of the word, are formed by the

---

7. I have not been able to trace the source of this quotation.
8. *Chāndogya Upaniṣad*, VI.8.7, in *The Principal Upaniṣads*, ed. and trans. S. Radhakrishnan. London: Allen and Unwin, 1953, p. 458.

linguistic speculations of the Indians, notably Patanjali (second century BCE) and Bhartrhari (fifth century CE). Rao himself observes:

> To say 'flower' . . . you must be able to say it in such a way that the force of the vocable has the power to create the flower. Unless word becomes mantra, no writer is a writer, and no reader a reader . . . We in India need but to recognize our inheritance. Let us never forget Bhartrhari.[9]

Mantra may be understood either as an instrument of thought (< Skt. *man*, to think + *tra*, a suffix used to make words denote instruments), or as salvific thought (< Skt. *man*, to think + *trai*, to save). In an oral culture, such as that of the Indians, thinking is done mnemonically to facilitate oral recurrence. Thought comes into existence in rhythmic, balanced patterns, in repetitions or antitheses, in epithetic, aphoristic or formulaic utterances, in proverbs or in other mnemonic forms. Words are therefore invested with power, and this relates them to the sacral, to the ultimate concerns of existence.

In examining Rao's use of English, it is important to keep in mind his philosophical and

---

9. Raja Rao, 'The Writer and the Word', *The Literary Criterion* 7.1 (Winter 1965): 231.

linguistic orientations. The house of fiction that he has built rests on these twin foundations. Among Indian writers in English he is perhaps unique in his attempt not only to nativize but also to Sanskritize the English language. Sanskritization is used here in the sense it is understood by anthropologists as a process of social and cultural change in Indian civilization. Rao strains to the limit all the expressive resources of the language. As a result, the Indian reality that emerges from his writing is authentic. Foremost among the problems the Indian writer has to wrestle with are, first, the expression of modes of thinking and feeling specific to his culture, and, second, terminology. Rao overcomes the first problem by invariably drawing upon Kannada and Sanskrit, and in the process he uses devices like loan translation, idiomatic and syntactic equivalences, and the imitation of native-style repertoires. He overcomes the second problem of finding words for culturally bound objects by contextualizing them so that their meanings are self-evident. By evoking the necessary cultural ambience, these strategies help the writer to be part of the mainstream of the literatures of India.

Among Kannada, Sanskrit, English and French, it is English that Rao most consummately possesses, and it is in that language that his fiction most consummately speaks to us. From the beginning, English is ritually de-anglicized. In *Kanthapura*, English is thick with the agglutinations of Kannada; in *The Serpent and the Rope*, the Indo-European kinship between English and Sanskrit is creatively exploited; and in *The Cat and Shakespeare*, English is made to approximate the rhythm of Sanskrit chants. At the apex of this linguistic pyramid is *The Chessmaster and His Moves*, wherein Rao has perfected an idiolect uniquely and inimitably his own. It is the culmination of his experiments with the English language spanning more than fifty years. *The Chessmaster and His Moves* has none of the self-consciousness in the use of English that characterizes his other work. In it he realizes the style that had eluded him in *The Serpent and the Rope*. Of style, he writes:

> The style of a man . . . the way he weaves word against word, intricates the existence of sentences with the values of *sound*, makes a comma here, puts a dash there: all are signs of the inner movement, the speed of his life, his breath (*prana*), the nature of his thought, the ardour and age of his soul. (1960: 164–65)

A peasant society such as Kanthapura has a homogeneous outlook and tradition. Its relationship to tradition produces a sense of unity and continuity between the present and past generations. Tradition is therefore an important instrument in ensuring social interdependence. Under the Raj, even villages were not spared the blessings of Pax Britannica, which triggered socio-economic changes that eventually split up the small communities. The oral tradition itself became fragmented, though it remained the chronicler of the motherland through a poetically gifted individual's repertoire.

Kanthapura is a mine of information about the sociocultural life of peasant society in southern India in the twentieth century. This is usually the perspective from which the novel is read in the West—the little tradition pitted against the great tradition, to use the terms proposed by Robert Redfield.[10] Redfield distinguishes the beliefs and practices of the folk from those of the elite in an agrarian society. The little tradition functions as a symbolic criticism of the great tradition, while at the same time gravitating towards it because of the latter's institutional charisma. Brahmins, for instance, who sit atop the caste hierarchy,

---

10. Robert Redfield, *Peasant Society and Culture: An Anthropological Approach to Civilization*. Chicago: University of Chicago Press, 1956, pp. 67–104.

owe their status to the belief that they alone are empowered to perform the *samskaras*, the central rituals of Hinduism. The recognition by the peasants of a great tradition, of which their practices are a variant, implies a stratification of culture. In a complex society such as India, the stratification of culture implies a stratification of power and wealth. The representatives of the great tradition are the gentry, officials and priests who collectively form a ruling as well as a cultural elite. Relations between the little and great traditions are uneasy and fraught with tension as their interests are diametrically opposed. The existing cultural hierarchy relegates the peasantry to a status of permanent inferiority. The little tradition lacks the institutional means for a direct confrontation with the great tradition. Colonialism further increased the distance between the little and great traditions by diluting ethnic identities.

The preface to *Kanthapura* is again a criticism not only of the language of the middle class but also of its ethnic identity and culture, which are fragmented. This is characteristic of societies under exploitative colonial regimes. The condition gives rise to social protest. In *Kanthapura*, under the influence of Gandhi, social protest becomes, on the one hand, a movement to reform the inegalitarian Indian society and, on the other, a movement to end British colonialism. The protest manifests itself as the expression of a critical attitude towards existing institutions and their underlying ethos. Social protest may be initiated by an individual or a community. Individuals, especially charismatic leaders such as Gandhi, play a decisive role in expressing social protest and mobilizing collective support for it.

Space within an Indian village is cut up and allocated to the different castes. Social relationships are interpersonal but hierarchical, with the Brahmin and the pariah at the opposite ends of the spectrum. Into this world steps a young Brahmin, Moorthy, who is educated in the town and is therefore considered modern. He is a figure of authority because he combines in himself upper-caste status and a college education. He is also a Gandhian and committed, like Gandhi, to ending British rule as well as the inequalities within Indian society such as untouchability and the oppression of women. The Gandhian movement was based on satyagraha ('firmness in truth'). Gandhi added an ethical dimension to what was basically a social and political movement. The Gandhian bias is obvious: moral revolution takes precedence over social and political revolutions. It is significant that Moorthy enters the Untouchable's house in his own village first, before his imprisonment as a revolutionary. While the inspiration of the novel is moral and humanistic, its idiom is spiritual and religious. Stress is laid on such values as righteousness, love, non-violence and on ritual beliefs and practices.

Kanthapura is one long, oral tale told in retrospect. There are other tales, interspersed with the main narrative, that begin with the oral tags, 'Once upon a time' and 'And this is how it all began', but these are usually digressions. Other characteristics of the oral narrative include the use of songs and prayers, proverbs, mythology, and epic lists and catalogues. In fact, the novel is unthinkable without the oral tradition. The preface itself defines *Kanthapura* as an oral—not a written—text.

> It may have been told of an evening, when as the dusk falls, and through the sudden quiet, lights leap up in house after house, and stretching her bedding on the veranda, a grandmother might have told you, newcomer, the sad tale of her village. (1963: viii)

It is within the frame of Kannada that the tale is told. English is made to simulate the 'thought-movement' and idiom of the old woman Achakka, who is the narrator. One detects here the notion of linguistic relativity associated with the Sapir–Whorf hypothesis that one's conceptualization of the world is partly the product of the form of the language habitually used to describe it and talk about it. Rao's use of English suggests the appropriation of the structural characteristics of Kannada, as Janet Powers Gemmill shows.[11] Consider the opening sentence as an example of syntactic re-creation:

> High on the Ghats is it, high up the steep mountains that face the cool Arabian seas, up the Malabar coast is it, up Mangalore and Puttur and many a centre of cardamom and coffee, rice and sugarcane. (1963: 1)

Gemmill has this translated into Kannada and again retranslated into English as follows:

> Upon ghats upon is it, upon steep mountain(s) upon, cool Arabian sea to face making mountain upon, Malabar coast upon is it, Mangalore, Puttur and many

---

11. Janet Powers Gemmill, 'The Transcreation of Spoken Kannada in Raja Rao's *Kanthapura*', *Literature East and West* 18.2–4 (1974): 191–202.

cardamom, coffee, rice, sugarcane centre(s) upon is.[12]

The similarity in the word order is unmistakable, especially the reversal of the word order of subject and verb, and the omission of the verb in the second clause. The deviation is of course kept within the bounds of intelligibility. The embedding of Kannada structure in English is done with such finesse as to be almost unnoticeable.

Parataxis and simple coordination are syntactic features that generally characterize the oral narrative. They dominate *Kanthapura*. One example will suffice—the celebrated description of the Kartik festival.

Kartik has come to Kanthapura, sisters— Kartik has come with the glow of lights and the unpressed footsteps of the wandering gods . . . and gods walked by lighted streets, blue gods and quiet gods and bright-eyed gods, and even as they walk in transparent flesh the dust gently sinks back to the earth, and many a child in Kanthapura sits late into the night to see the crown of this god and that god, and how many a god has chariots

12. Gemmill, 'The Transcreation of Spoken Kannada in Raja Rao's *Kanthapura*', p. 194.

with steeds white as foam and queens so
bright that the eyes shut themselves in fear
lest they be blinded. (1963: 81)

Idioms are a fertile area for nativization, and
here, Rao both transplants from Kannada and
implants new ones; e.g., 'To stitch up one's mouth'
(1963: 58); 'to tie one's daughter to the neck of'
(1963: 35); 'a crow-and-sparrow story' (1963: 15)
(from 'a cock-and-bull story'); and 'every squirrel
has his day' (1963: 77) (from 'every dog has his
day').

Adjuncts are frequently used in oral narratives
for highlighting a word or phrase; e.g., 'And the
Swami, who is he?' (1963: 41); '[M]y heart, it beat
like a drum' (1963: 182); 'She has never failed us,
I assure you, our Kenchamma' (1963: 2); and 'Our
village—Kanthapura is its name' (1963: 1).

In an Indian village, relationships are
interpersonal. Social stratification is along
the lines of caste and occupation. Often,
idiosyncrasies and physical disabilities attach
themselves as sobriquets to the names of
individuals. Examples of these abound in the
novel: Patel Rangè Gowda, Pariah Sidda, Post-
office Suryanarayana, Husking Rangi, Four-
beamed-house Chandrasekharayya, One-eyed
Linga, and Waterfall Venkamma.

On ceremonial occasions, social relationships are meticulously observed. In a traditional society, certain aspects of conversation are ritualized. Elaborate attention is paid, for example, to modes of address. They reflect the use of language as a means of establishing a friendly rapport between speaker and listener and of reinforcing communal solidarity. For instance, in a host–guest interactional situation, Rao hits upon the exact phrase translated from Kannada to dispel any uneasiness. The guest is coaxed: 'Take it Bhattarè, only one cup more, just one? Let us not dissatisfy our manes' (1963: 21). On the anniversary of a death in a Brahmin family, other Brahmins are invited to a feast, and they are expected to indulge their appetites fully, so that the spirits of the dead are pacified. C.D. Narasimhaiah remarks: 'With a people like us, used to being coaxed, the English form, "Won't you have a second helping?", or the mere "Sure you don't care for more?" will be ineffective, and even considered discourteous.'[13] Culture-sensitive situations like these are not always understood.

---

13. C.D. Narasimhaiah, 'Indian Writing in English: An Introduction', *The Journal of Commonwealth Literature* 5 (1968): 14.

Through a choice of strategies, skilfully deployed, Rao has been able to reconstruct the performance-oriented discourse of the traditional oral tales of India. Kanthapura is village India in microcosm—the context that has determined and shaped the expressive devices in the novel.

Rao considers his entire work as:

> An attempt at puranic recreation of Indian storytelling: that is to say, the story, as story, is conveyed through a thin thread to which are attached (or which passes through) many other stories, fables, and philosophical disquisitions, like a mala (garland).[14]

Philosophical debates are a part of both the Upanishads and the puranas. *The Serpent and the Rope* resembles both. The novel interprets Vedanta in terms of the discourse of fiction. The philosophy is not an interpolation. It is an integral part of the novel, its informing principle.

In the spirit of the Upanishads, the novel attempts to inquire into the nature of the Self and the attainment of Self-Knowledge

---

14. Quoted in M.K. Naik, *Raja Rao*. Twayne World Authors Series. New York: Twayne, 1972, p. 106.

with the help of the Guru. The protagonist, Ramaswamy, is an aspirant in this spiritual quest. In the process, he has to tear through the veil of ignorance (*avidya*). He explains the quest with the help of an analogy—that of the serpent and the rope—that Sankara himself uses.

> The world is either unreal or real—the serpent or the rope. There is no in-between-the-two—and all that's in-between is poetry, is sainthood . . . For wheresoever you go, you see only with the serpent's eyes. Whether you call it duality or modified duality . . . you look at the rope from the posture of the serpent, you feel you are the serpent—you are the rope. But in true fact, with whatever eyes you see there is no serpent, there never was a serpent . . . One—the Guru—brings you the lantern; the road is seen, the long, white road, going with the statutory stars. 'It's only the rope.' He shows it to you. (1960: 333)

A powerful recursive device used throughout the novel is the dash (–) to suggest the to-and-fro movement of a thought, its amplitude and density. And this passage is a good example of it. The dash is used to indicate a break or an interruption in the thought. In between dashes, a thought is often insinuated or slipped under the breath, as it were.

Before Ramaswamy is on the 'long, white road' to Travancore that would lead him to the Guru, his life takes many twists and turns. His marriage to Madeleine, whom he meets while a student in France, breaks up, especially after Savithri comes into his life. Savithri is the eldest daughter of Raja Raghubir Singh of Surajpur, and Ramaswamy meets her on a visit to India. Savithri is the woman he has been waiting for; but she is soon to be married to his friend Pratap.

Ramaswamy's relationship with Savithri is reinforced by the myth of the princess Savithri as told in 'The Book of the Forest' (the *Vanaparvan*) of the Mahabharata. Savithri is a *pativrata*, a woman who observes the vow of devotion to her husband. Indian tradition ascribes extraordinary powers to a chaste wife. Her marriage to Satyavan is doomed from the start. Her husband is to die within a year. Yama, the god of death, arrives at the end of the year to claim Satyavan. Refusing to give up on her husband, Savithri takes on Yama and wins him over by strictly observing her dharma. Through her love and devotion, Savithri rescues Satyavan from Yama himself. In the novel, Savithri likewise rescues Ramaswamy from inertia and puts him on the spiritual path. Alone now, Ramaswamy calls out: 'Not a God but a Guru is what I need' (1960: 400). And the Guru appears in a vision: 'He called me, and said, "It is so long, so long, my son. I have awaited you. Come, we go . . ." To such a Truth was I taken, and became its servant, I kissed the perfume of its Holy Feet, and called myself a disciple' (1960: 401).

If Kannada is the prototype for English in *Kanthapura*, it is Sanskrit in *The Serpent and the Rope*. Sanskrit is the obvious choice, as the novel has a strong metaphysical bias. It was in Sanskrit that the philosophical speculations of the Indians found their profoundest expression. Rao's Sanskritic English is not unlike Milton's Latinate English in *Paradise Lost*. The intent is the same: to assimilate into English the qualities and features of a prestigious language the writer admires most. As opposed to the Prakrits, the vernaculars, Sanskrit was the 'perfected' language. The Sanskritization of English should be seen as part of a wider sociocultural phenomenon that has historically characterized Indian civilization. Louis Dumont and David Pocock interpret Sanskritization as the 'acceptance of a more distinguished or prestigious way of saying the same things'.[15] Quotations in the original,

---

15. Louis Dumont and David Pocock, 'On the Different Aspects or Levels in Hinduism', *Contributions to Indian Sociology* 3 (July 1959): 45.

together with English translations from the classical Sanskrit poets—Kalidasa (fourth–fifth century) and Bhavabhuti (eighth century)—and from the devotional hymns of Sankara and Mira (sixteenth century), are skilfully woven into the story and function as a parallel text. Ramaswamy relapses into Sanskrit to tell Madeleine as delicately as possible what he is unable to tell her openly—his feeling of despair as she increasingly withdraws into herself. He finds a parallel in Bhavabhuti's *Uttararāmacarita* ('The Later Story of Rama'), to which he draws her attention. The occasion has all the solemnity of a ritual, and it represents his farewell to her.

> *ekaḥ samprati nāśitapriyatamastāmadye rāmaḥ*
> *katham|*
> *pāpaḥ pañcavatīṃ vilokayatu vā gacchatvasaṃ*
> *bhāvya vā||* (II. 28) (1960: 326)

Alone, now, after being the cause of the loss of his dear [wife], how should Rama, sinful as he is, visit that very same Pāncavatī, or how pass on regardless of it?[16]

---

16. Bhavabhuti, *Rama's Later History* (*Uttararāmacarita*), part 1: Introduction and Translation by Shripad Krishna Belvalkar. Harvard Oriental Series, 21. Cambridge, MA: Harvard University Press, 1915, p. 39.

The philosophical bias is even more pronounced in *The Cat and Shakespeare*. Rao exploits the Advaita Vedantic idea of the world being a play (*lila*) of the Absolute, and the result is an exhilarating comedy. However, it is the Visishta Advaita ('qualified monism') Vedanta of Ramanuja (eleventh–twelfth century) that informs the novel. Ramanuja emphasizes the way of devotion (*bhakti-marga*) to God in which the seeker surrenders himself to His grace to achieve salvation. This is seen in the two schools that developed after Ramanuja: the 'Northern School' (*Vadagalai*) and the 'Southern School' (*Tengalai*). According to the first, salvation is achieved by following the 'analogy of the monkey' (*markata-nyaya*). Just as the young one of a monkey feels safe when it holds on to its mother's body, so does God save those who make an effort to reach Him. According to the second, salvation is achieved by following the 'analogy of the cat' (*marjara-nyaya*). Just as a kitten is carried by a cat in its teeth, so does God save those who do not even make an effort to reach Him.

It is Govindan Nair, the protagonist Ramakrishna Pai's neighbour, who best exemplifies the 'analogy of the cat' in the novel. Both Nair and Pai are civil servants in the former princely state of Travancore in south-western India e early 1940s. The Second World War is on.

The kitten is being carried by the cat. We would all be kittens carried by the cat. Some, who are lucky . . . will one day know it . . . Ah, the kitten when its neck is held by its mother, does it know anything else but the joy of being held by its mother? You see the elongated thin hairy thing dangling, and you think, poor kid, it must suffer to be so held. But I say the kitten is the safest thing in the world, the kitten held in the mouth of the mother cat. Could one have been born without a mother? . . . But a mother—I tell you, without Mother the world is not. So allow her to fondle you and to hold you.[17]

As a clerk in Ration Office No. 66 in Trivandrum, Nair earns forty-five rupees a month. He has little or no prospect of becoming rich. His son, Shridhar, dies from pneumonia, and he has a brush with the law that lands him in prison. But none of this affects Nair. He remains his usual optimistic self, with a firm belief in the mother cat. His faith saves him in the end.

Pai, as a clerk in the Revenue Board, dreams of building a three-storeyed house. A Saraswat

17. Raja Rao, *The Cat and Shakespeare*. New York: Macmillan, 1965, pp. 8-10. Subsequent citations from this edition are indicated in the text parenthetically by page number.

Brahmin, he enters into a relationship with a Nair woman, Shantha, a schoolteacher. This is a social custom known as *sambandham* ('relationship') that was once prevalent in Kerala among the Nairs. Pai's wife, Saroja, has no say in the matter. She removes herself to her ancestral home, Kartikura House, in Alwaye with her son, Vithal. 'What is woman, you may ask. Well, woman is Shantha,' says Pai, and goes on, 'Shantha also loves . . . she is so exquisite in her love play. She is shy like a peahen. Her giving is complete' (1965: 20–21). But the 'dearest thing' in Pai's life is his five-year-old daughter, Usha. Both Shantha and Usha embody the feminine principle as does the Mother Cat (a symbol for the compassionate Guru). They are the instruments of divine grace (*kripa*). For, in the *Kulacūḍāmaṇi Nigama* ('The Crest-Jewel of the Kula Doctrine'), a tantric text in praise of the goddess Shakti, we learn that even Shiva cannot become the supreme Lord unless Shakti unites with Him. And from Their union, all things arise. Shakti in fact says, 'I manifest Myself as woman which is My own Self and the very essence of creation in order to know You, Shiva, the Guru, who are united with Me.'[18]

---

18. Arthur Avalon, ed. *Kulacūḍāmaṇi Nigama*, with an introduction and translation by A.K. Maitra. Madras: Ganesh & Co., 1956, ch. 1, verses 25–26.

Like Govindan Nair, Pai too has his moment of illumination.

> I saw truth not as fact but as ignition. I could walk into fire and be cool, I could sing and be silent, I could hold myself and yet not be there . . . I smelled a breath that was of nowhere but rising in my nostrils sank back into me, and found death was at my door. I woke up and found death had passed by, telling me I had no business to be there. Then where was I? Death said it had died. I had killed death. When you see death as death, you kill it. (1965: 113–14)

Again, the British presence in India is inescapable; it is reinforced by the ubiquitous presence of the English language. And what better representative of English can there be than Shakespeare himself? Rao's coupling of Shakespeare and the cat in the title is ironic. Both Sankara and Ramanuja wrote their influential works in Sanskrit, the *deva-vani*, 'the language of the gods'. Now, English, the new *deva-vani*, has replaced Sanskrit as the lingua franca. And Rao himself, unable to write in Sanskrit, writes in English. The irony is directed at himself. In the novel, Nair revels in Shakespearean locutions. Unable to rid themselves of the British, Indians retreat into the past, finding solace in religion and philosophy. Rao's 'Tale of India' could not have been more timely. It points to India's impoverishment as an enslaved nation.

The Cat and Shakespeare exhibits none of the communicative strategies of *Kanthapura* or *The Serpent and the Rope*. Unlike the highly individual and expressive idiolects of the earlier novels, that of *The Cat and Shakespeare* is deliberately ordinary, since the intent is to express traditional lore. In this process, Rao has pitted the symmetry of language against the asymmetry of thought with its indirections and paradoxes. The highly reductive style of *The Cat and Shakespeare* is in strong contrast to the expansiveness of the other novels.

Raja Rao's short stories reveal him as a master who extended the possibilities of the genre. In his hands, the form becomes an instrument of metaphysical inquiry that transforms the language into true poetry.

First published in 1933 in *Asia*, New York, when Rao was only twenty-five, 'Javni' has attained the status of a classic. The epigraph from Kanakadasa, a sixteenth-century Kannada devotional poet, suggests the theme of the story: the relationship between an English-educated boy, Ramu, a Brahmin, and a low-caste servant,

Javni, a widow, who works for his married sister, Sita. The story is a plea for women's emancipation and the abolition of the caste system. Ramu and Javni share the same religious nature, his at the level of metaphysics, and hers in a belief in spirits and simple devotion to the goddess Talakamma. Ramu sees himself as an instrument of social change that breaks down the barriers of caste. Talking to Javni, Ramu experiences a kind of epiphany in which he sees her as a divine being, a great soul. This mood, of course, does not last, and Ramu accepts the distinctions of caste between them as the family moves away two years later. He accepts the fact that Javni is but a servant who must be left behind. He universalizes her and sees her as one with the sky and the river. His mental act is in keeping with Indian metaphysics: man is seen to be one with nature, his apparent separateness being nothing but an illusion.

Ramu's initial indignation at Sita's treatment of Javni is replaced by admiration and later by acceptance of the social demands of caste. Javni's eating in the byre is the source of conflict between Ramu and Sita. Sita sees the mixing of castes as irreligious, while Ramu sees putting Javni with the cows as inhuman. Sita cannot transcend her caste.

Time and again I had quarrelled with my sister about it all. But she would not argue with me. 'They are of the lower class, and you cannot ask them to sit and eat with you,' she would say.[19]

Throughout the story, Javni is identified with the cow; for example, 'Javni, she is good like a cow' (1978: 86). Later, the identification between Javni and the cow is complete when we are told that 'Javni sat in the dark, swallowing mouthfuls of rice that sounded like a cow chewing the cud' (1978: 88). In her cow-like way, Javni accepts the teaching of the dominant caste and learns to live with the discomfort imposed by caste distinctions. Ramu recognizes in her the greatness that knows no caste and yet accepts the caste system. The cow functions as an expanding symbol that points to India's survival as a civilization, to Hinduism and its reverence for life (ahimsa), and to the transcendentalism of a world where the sacred is mixed with the profane. Ramu's awareness at the metaphysical level that there is no caste coexists with his social

19. Raja Rao, *The Policeman and the Rose: Stories*. Delhi: Oxford University Press, 1978, p. 88. Subsequent citations from this edition are indicated in the text parenthetically by page number.

acceptance that such distinctions do exist. 'No, Javni. In contact with a heart like yours, who will not bloom into a god?' (1978: 96).

Tagore's classic story of village India, 'The Postmaster' (1891), ends on a similar note. The orphan Ratan is abandoned by the postmaster, who finds life in the village of Ulapur intolerable and returns home to Calcutta. The postmaster is more than just an employer to her; he is a father figure, someone she respects and admires. He had provided her a home. For one brief period, his illness brings them together. Ratan rises to the occasion and is transformed from a girl into a young woman. So when Ratan asks him, '"Dada, will you take me to your home?" The postmaster laughed. "What an idea!" said he; but he did not think it necessary to explain to the girl wherein lay the absurdity.'[20] On leaving the village, the postmaster takes comfort in philosophic reflection: 'The grief-stricken face of a village girl seemed to represent for him the great unspoken pervading grief of Mother Earth herself.' (1918: 124) Abandoned by their families, the Javnis and Ratans learn to fend

---

20. Rabindranath Tagore, *Stories from Tagore*. New York: Macmillan, 1918, p. 122. Subsequent citations from this edition are indicated in the text parenthetically by page number.

for themselves in an inhospitable world. Both stories underscore the resilience of the Indian woman under stress.

'Nimka' was first published in *The Illustrated Weekly of India*, Bombay, in 1963. Set in Paris in the first half of the twentieth century, the story reveals the extent of Rao's immersion in European culture. Himself an exile in France, the narrator, an Indian student at the Sorbonne, is able to sympathize with Nimka's plight as a White Russian émigré who flees her homeland in the wake of the Bolshevik Revolution of 1917. Attracted to Nimka, the narrator goes into raptures over her beauty: 'Her beauty had certainty, it had a rare equilibrium, and a naughtiness that was feminine and very innocent . . . It was beauty—it always will be, and you cannot take it, and as such you cannot soil yourselves' (1978: 99).

Nimka's interest in India begins with her interest in the narrator. It expands thereafter to include Tolstoy's admiration of Gandhi, and stories from the epics, the Mahabharata and the Ramayana, especially the story of Nala and Damayanti from 'The Book of the Forest' (the *Vanaparvan*) of the Mahabharata. Nimka sees in Damayanti, the princess of Vidarbha, a reflection of her own unhappy life. But then she is no

Damayanti, and Count Vergilian Kormaloff, her husband, is no Nala, king of Nishadha. One misfortune after another strikes Nala and Damayanti: Nala loses his kingdom to his brother Pushkara in a game of dice, and lives in the forest with Damayanti, whom he later abandons; but in the end, he wins his kingdom back, and is reunited with Damayanti. Kormaloff loses his entire fortune betting on horses, abandons Nimka, and their son, Boris, and flees to Monte Carlo. When seventeen years old, Boris goes back to Russia and is never heard of again. Nimka's dream of returning to the Smolny courtyard in St Petersburg never materializes. She is all alone now. 'She asked nothing of life' (1978: 103).

The identification of the narrator with the swan in the story of Nala and Damayanti is significant. It is the swan that introduces Nala to Damayanti by praising the king's virtues; Damayanti falls in love with Nala and vows to marry only him.

> Nimka knew the Indian saying that the swan knows how to separate milk from water—the good from the bad, and as I knew her to be good, she recognized me a swan. The swan sailed in and out and India became the land where all that is wrong everywhere goes right there. (1978: 100)

The swan or bar-headed goose (*hamsa, Anser indicus*) is, in Indian iconography, a symbol of enlightenment, of those able to discern between the Self and the non-Self. The title *paramahamsa* ('supreme soul'; an ascetic of utmost sanctity) is often bestowed upon those who have become fully enlightened, such as Ramakrishna Paramahamsa (1836–86). Hamsa is also one of the names of Vishnu. Sankara writes: 'The Lord is called Hamsa as He dispels (*hanti*) the fear of transmigration for those who meditate upon the oneness of "I am He" (*aham sah*).'[21] The statement 'I am He' sums up the essential teaching of the Upanishads: the atman and Brahman are one and the same. Again, the bird features prominently in classical Sanskrit poetry. In Kalidasa's *Meghadūta* ('The Cloud Messenger'), the Yaksha, an exile in the Vindhya Mountains, tells the cloud that on its journey to Lake Manasa, carrying his message to his wife in their home in Alaka in the Himalaya, it will be accompanied by a flock of wild geese.

Eager to fly to Lake Manasa, a flock of wild geese,

---

21. Integral Yoga Institute, ed. *Dictionary of Sanskrit Names*. Yogaville, Buckingham, VA: Integral Yoga Publications, 1989, p. 57.

with shoots of lotus stalks to sustain them
on the journey, will be your companions
in the sky as far as Mount Kailasa.[22]

Rich in symbolism, the swan (wild goose)
weaves the stories of Nala and Damayanti, and the
Yaksha and his wife into the very fabric of 'Nimka',
deepening its resonance, and making the reader
aware of its metaphysical significance. Time and
space do not seem to matter as we uncover the
many layers of this unforgettable story.

The reunions of Nala and Damayanti, and of
the Yaksha and his wife, make Nimka's situation
all the more poignant. Is India then the 'land
where all that is wrong everywhere goes right
there'?

Though the narrator is involved in the story,
he also stands outside it. Perhaps he realizes
that Nimka is after all an illusion (maya). As
Michel reminds us: 'The object exists because
of its name. Remove the name, and the object
is space. Remove the space, and the object is
the Reality' (1978: 101-02). Is Nimka real or
unreal? She is a shadowy figure, a fantasy of the
narrator's imagination, someone ethereal who

22. Sushil Kumar De, ed., and Rev. V. Raghavan, *The
Meghadūta of Kālidāsa*, 3rd ed. New Delhi: Sahitya
Akademi, 1982, verse 11.

flits in and out of the story. In 'Nimka', Rao transcends the limits of the short story to explore states of consciousness that are not usually accessible to language by drawing upon, on the one hand, myths and folklore, and on the other, metaphysics, to try to express the inexpressible. By all accounts, 'Nimka' is a triumph.

The author's note to the reader asks that the eleven stories in *On the Ganga Ghat* 'be read as one single novel'. The scene is Kashi, the City of Light, with the ever-flowing Ganga in the background. This is the stage on which the stories are enacted. It seems that the entire world has gathered in Kashi as if for a festival. The Indian imagination is mythopoeic, and so gods and humans mingle with one another as story after story from Kashi's *sthala-purana* is woven seamlessly into the narrative. Like the ever-flowing Ganga, there is no end to the stories. It is for this reason that Rao would like us to consider the book as a 'single novel'.

Let us look at one of the stories, 'X' (the stories do not have titles)—that of Sudha, the only daughter of the jeweller Ranchoddoss Sunderdoss, whose family business was founded way back in 1799 on Girgaum Road in Bombay.

They say on the day she was born, suddenly,
a peacock, wings outstretched and keening,

strutted past the courtyard (the mother had gone to Kathiawar, to her own mother, for the childbirth) and everybody said: 'Well, this girl, she will bring in holy riches.'[23]

At fourteen, Sudha resolves not to marry. She would sit for hours in the family sanctuary, chanting 'Rama, Sri Rama'. She would even fast and observe days of silence. One night she has a vision: 'a sadhu would come to initiate her, and she would then become a true devotee of the Lord' (1993: 113). In three days, a handsome south Indian sadhu arrives at the Ranchoddoss's and asks Sudha's mother, Ramabehn: 'Is there anyone living in this house who's deeply devoted to the Lord?' (1993: 114). On hearing this, Sudha comes out and falls at the sadhu's feet. At that moment, she remembers her past life 'somewhere in Kathiawar'. After three months, the sadhu initiates her into sannyas ('life as a wandering ascetic'). Sudha puts on a white sari, and a few days later leaves with the sadhu for the Himalaya. Ramabehn is devastated and dies, and Ranchoddoss leaves home in search of

_____

23. Raja Rao, *On the Ganga Ghat*. Delhi: Orient Paperbacks, 1993, p. 112. Subsequent citations from this edition are indicated in the text parenthetically by page number.

his daughter. He finds her in Benares, reading the *Vāsiṣṭha Rāmāyaṇa* to widows and ascetics. '"Father," she said, looking at the flowing Ganga before her, "Father, I think I have just a chink to the door of Knowledge—to Jnan"' (1993: 120). Happy to be reunited with his daughter, Ranchoddoss begins his spiritual exercises in earnest under her guidance. Later, father and daughter visit Badrinath to see her guru's guru (her own guru, the sadhu, had died). The Guru initiates Ranchoddoss into sannyas. 'Life flows as you see, like the Ganga herself . . . reminding you that the Truth is but one indivisible flow. What is dream and which reality, then?' (1993: 120). Ranchoddoss, the jeweller from Bombay, understands. He has at last come home.

Sankara praises the river in his 'Hymn to Ganga' ('Gangāstotraṃ'):

> Rather a fish or a turtle in Thy waters,
> A tiny lizard on Thy bank, would I be,
> Or even a shunned and hated outcaste
> Living but a mile from Thy sacred stream,
> Than the proudest emperor afar from Thee.[24]

---

24. Sankara, *Ātmabodhaḥ: Self-Knowledge*, trans. Swami Nikhilananda. Madras: Sri Ramakrishna Math, 1967, p. 261, verse 11.

The true protagonist of these stories are not the men and women who throng the ghats of Kashi, but the Ganga herself. Like a thread of gold, the river braids the stories into a seamless whole. *On the Ganga Ghat* is steeped in the spiritual life of Kashi and is an eloquent reminder of the centrality of the city and the river in the Indian consciousness.

What is remarkable about these three stories is Rao's understanding of women. Javni, Nimka and Sudha come across as real people whom we may have known. They are not characters in fiction. Sudha's story is especially poignant. Born into a wealthy family, she gives up a life of ease and privilege. A spiritual aspirant, she leaves home and goes forth into homelessness in search of, as her name implies, the nectar of Knowledge.

It was Rao, who, more than any other writer of his generation—which included Mulk Raj Anand (1905-2004) and R.K. Narayan (1906-2001)—established the status of Indian literature in English during India's struggle for independence from British rule. Neither Anand nor Narayan had come anywhere close to Rao's innovative approach to fiction. Rao's fiction is a philosophical quest in search of the word as mantra that would lead to liberation. Rao never considered himself to be solely an Indian writer. He had spent his formative years in France and not in England. Though his novels are rooted in the Indian philosophical tradition, they are universal in scope. Rao was conscious of the fact that English is an Indo-European language and therefore distantly related to Sanskrit. In his fiction, English, French and Sanskrit rub shoulders with one another in a linguistic family reunion of sorts. What is explored is the nature of language itself in an attempt to know the Truth.

The English language does not have sufficiently deep roots in India. It is therefore important for the writer to find his own individual style through which to express his world view. The reader, on his part, if he is not to misread the text, must get to know the writer's epistemological viewpoint, or the sum total of beliefs, preconceptions and values which the writer shares with others within a sociocultural context.

R. Parathasarathy
Saratoga Springs, New York
15 January 2014

AUTHOR'S NOTE

'Two plus two makes four' is commonplace arithmetic. 'When you take away plentitude (*purnasya*) from plentitude, what remains over is plentitude' is an ancient Upanishadic saying. The problem of meaning is not what you say but from where you say it. Man-centered explications at best end in dithyrambic numbers, in sociological aesthetics, and Truth-turned discourse leads one to silence and so to meaning. The two seem complimentary but in fact the first is exclusive of the second, whereas, not so the second of the first. My friend Govindan Nair (whom you will soon meet) is no enemy of Kirillov (whom you all know) but Govindan Nair is, alas, good Kirillov's. It is a pity, therefore, that Govindan Nair did not meet Kirillov. It would have been such fun, and—who knows—Govindan Nair might yet have charmed Kirillov into his unbeginning game.

Plentitude has no quarrel with two, but two is the enemy of plentitude. And so of Shakespeare. The not-two alone is meaning in any meaning: 'Truth is the meaning of the lie for meaning is Truth,' etc., etc. Truth alone is position-less, so you play. The two (plus two) ends in suicide. I like play. So let us play. Come, Kirillov, let us play chess, you and I.

I have a small white house here, with a courtyard. From the back I look over coconut trees, and huts, and somewhere there's the sound of the sea.

I was appointed divisional clerk, Trivandrum, some two years ago. I left my wife and two children at Pattanur. My eldest was five years of age, my youngest three. It's not so easy to change schools, you know; and then it was monsoon time. When I thought of the bad new road (which leads to Kamla Bhavan, the noble name my fat landlord inflicted on this blue and ochre-banded building), I suffered to think of Usha coming back from school in this mess. Usha has sensitive hands, and her schoolmistress Tangamma was always telling her: Child,

1

you have the fingers to make a nice braid. You will be a dutiful wife. My wife Saroja said: 'Nice thing for teachers to be talking of wives already.' But that is the way with my wife. She cannot help all the time talking of the wife. I am a quiet man, and to speak the truth, I don't yet know what it is to mean husband.

Yes, at last I had a house. It was new and it was white. It had ochre bands on it—almost as on a temple—and I could hear the sea.

Now that the monsoon was as its fiercest, there was a problem even about going to the office. I ate every day at the Home Friends; the food was bad, but the freedom was so good. When I did not eat at the Home Friends, I could always go to the Trivandrum Brahmins' Hotel. There the food smells less bad but the place looks more untidy. Life is always this choice—to choose an old house nearer the office or the new one sitting amidst coconut gardens. My wife saw this and said: 'Oh, it's just like home, coconut trees, huts, and the sound of the sea.' For she is from Alwaye. And she never tired of saying how her old grandfather spoke of the way the Dutch landed some two hundred years ago, and thank heavens the Kartikuras' house was two miles inland—but you could hear the sea—and the Dutch took away all the able-bodied men to fight (or to become Christians), and Kartikura House, being two miles inland, was left in peace. So the two miles and the coconut trees saved the Kartikura people, and thus emerged my wife, and from her and me, Usha and Vithal, my last born, a boy so round and fresh, with a *tilak* on his brow, and he leaps when he sees a car, and says, 'Take me on a pom-pom,' but I make him ride on my knee. But here, in Trivandrum, I sit alone and ride my own knee, as it were. I like being alone. I like eating *dose* and drinking coffee at Jyothibhavan. 'Hey, take this away, this is such bad coffee,' you can always say to the Brahmin boy, but you cannot say that to Saroja. She will talk of the Dutch and Christianity—and the sea.

The Dutch of course are an able-bodied people who have white ships. I have seen them because I have been to Bombay. During the war I tried to get into the navy and have better emoluments. At the interview they made me sit and leap so much, I cried, 'Ay ya yo yo,' and said: 'No more silver than this hand can earn driving a nib.' A man is meant to work for his wife, to feed her, and for the children to go to school (I so much liked Usha coming back along the railway embankment from school—three miles are three good miles from Pattanur to Alwaye, but then there's the signal, the red and green lights, and all the other children, and father at home. Vithal was, of course, always in his mother's arms).

I was thirty-three, and I had ever wondered that one is alive. I wanted to become a rich man, for then my wife would be so happy that I could do what I liked. If my plans went well—and in the new India plans are never so difficult, the new is made with plans—I would build a big house, like contractor Srinivasa Pai. He is some distant cousin of mine, and I no more like his house than I like his face. But people usually introduce me in the office saying, 'This is Mr Ramakrishna Pai, cousin of Srinivasa Pai of Chalai Bazaar,' as if I belonged to some royal lineage. My lineage smells of chilli and cardamom and

4

tamarind as my wife's does of coconuts. But then my wife's people had two or three boats that plied the canals, and banditry and pilfering can make a lot of difference with prices. One can build a Kartikura House on thuggery. My wife was the second child; the first daughter was amply given away to a merchant in Ernakulam. Sundari (my wife's sister) must tell Ramu, her husband, about the Dutch and the sea. Ernakulam must have many ruins and the Dutch must have left a few guns there. In Kartikura House they still show you Dutch cannon balls. When you plough for the tapioca sowings, the cannon balls come out just like the tapioca. Usha used to say, 'The cannon is hard tapioca but this tapioca is man's.' Thus the cannon became the gods'. Strange how we transform all things into ours. Our houses must look like us, just as our ancestors built temples in the shape of man. In Chidamabaram Temple, Shankar Iyer says, the image of Shiva occupies the place of the heart. Then what is the place Parwathi[1] occupies? I sometimes

---

1. Wife of Shiva and daughter of Himalaya.

wonder whether I have a heart as I wonder in summer whether the rains will ever come. In heat I strike. I struck my wife only twice and have left marks on her face.

I don't know if you've heard of a *bilva* tree—it has three leaves and a crust of thick thorns. It's a scraggy tree but dear to Shiva, for one night a hunter trying to shoot at his game—was it a deer or a porcupine?—went up this obnoxious stump, and in his hours of waiting, sent down leaf after leaf, so they say, and a Shiva image being beneath, Shiva himself came in a vision and said: 'Here I am.' For it's not the way you worship that is important but what you adore. Even an accidental fall of leaves on Shiva's head got the wicked hunter his vision. And thus the stump of tree became sacred—and its trefoil sacred, for all that is sacred to God.

So when I look from my window eastwards, just by the garden wall, I see this stump of *bilva* tree, thorns visible in the morning sun. And I wonder if God will ever bless me, just like that.

Vithal would have to go to school next year, I was saying to myself one vacant morning. Usha would have to be brought to Trivandrum and sent to the convent. The sisters there, you know, are Belgian, they say, and very good. They teach excellent English— and never forget they also teach Malayalam. But then for a Saraswath Brahmin[2] like me, Malayalam or English is all the same. The Revenue Board has no preference, or if preferences there be, they lie in the direction of English. But soon it will be Hindi, and my Konkani will be of help. God helps one in everything. Will I build a big house? That is what I asked looking at the tree.

Just at that moment Govindan Nair looks up from between the leaves and says: 'Hey there, be you at home?' That is his style, if one may say so, of talking. It's a mixture of *The Vicar of Wakefield* and Shakespeare. The words are choice, the choice of the situation clumsy. He never says come and

2. Brahmins who fled, so it is believed, from persecution in Kashmir during the early years of Muslim conquest. In Travancore, they are mostly engaged in business. Their language is Konkani, which is akin to Hindi.

go. He will always say: 'Gentleman, may I invite myself there? Will I be permitted into your presence?' That's ever the way with him, in English or in Malayalam. He must twist a thing into its essence and spread it out. So that milk becomes cow's precious liquid or water the aqua of Ganges. His heart is so big, it builds a wall lest it runs away with everything. He always wants to run away with everything. In fact he himself is . . . running.

I have hardly formulated this in my slow mind—for as you can see, I am just like that hunter carelessly dropping *bilva* leaves on some Shiva as yet unknown—when this big creature Govindan Nair leaps across the wall. That he is round and tall makes no difference to his movements. The fact is, to him all the world is just what he does. He does and so the world comes into being. He himself calls it: 'The kitten is being carried by the cat. We would all be kittens carried by the cat. Some, who are lucky (like your hunter), will one day know it. Others live hearing "meow-meow". . . . I like being the kitten. And how about you, sir?' he would say. Then he would

8

spread his fat legs on my bench, open his paws, produce some betel leaf or tobacco (or a cheap cigarette, if that could be found, but this almost never before me, for he knows I hate lighted tobacco), and munching his munch and massaging his limbs, he opens his discourse. 'I tell you, Ramakrishna Pai, there's nothing like becoming rich. Our wives adore us if we can produce a car, even a toy car for the baby. Females have one virtue. They adore gilt. My wife is from a grand family. But I am a poor clerk like you. Of course, I did brilliant things when I was young—I was handsome and all that, mothers used to tell me, and I rode a B.S.A. bicycle. I wore grey flannels and went to the College Tennis Club. For I do know of girls. Then some big man thought I was going to be a big man. And thus the wife came into existence. And two children to boot. But the great man became big in fact, and his clerkship remained at forty-five rupees. Fortunately there are wars. And rationing is one of the grandest inventions of man. You stamp paper with figures and you feed stomachs on numbers. I was such, I am such, an original figure. You know there

9

are sadhus, so they say, for I am ignorant of such things, who are supposed to eat three pinches of sand one day, and the mantra[3] does the rest. For three months they need no food. I am such a sadhu, dispensing numbers. I give magical cards, and my wife eats pearl rice. My children go to school. My father-in-law lives on his estates and says: "Hey, clerk, what about my daughter?" I laugh. A clerk is a clerk. He could at best rise to the post of superintendent and have two peons at his door. Isn't that so, dear sir? Ah, the kitten when its neck is held by its mother, does it know anything else but the joy of being held by its mother? You see the elongated thin hairy thing dangling, and you think, poor kid, it must suffer to be so held. But I say the kitten is the safest thing in the world, the kitten held in the mouth of the mother cat. Could one have been born without a mother? Modern inventions do not so much need a father. But a mother—I tell you, without Mother the world is not. So allow her to fondle you and to hold you. I often think how noble it is to

---

3. The recitation of sacred syllables.

see the world, the legs dangling straight, the eyes steady, and the mouth of the mother at the neck. Beautiful.' Then Govindan Nair would go off on a quiet silence munching his betel leaves. 'You are an innocent. I tell you God will build you a house of three storeys— note, please, I say three storeys—here, just where you sit. It's already there. You've just to look and see, look deep and see. Let the mother cat hold you by the neck. Suppose I were for a moment to show you the mother cat!' Govindan Nair never says anything indifferent. For him all gestures, all words have absolute meaning. 'I meow-meow the dictionary, but my meaning is always one,' he used to assure me.

'And so?'

'And so, sir, let us build a house of three storeys here. I am in the rationing department, and you in the Revenue Board. Figures, magical be figures in wartime. And you build a house, and like in some hospitals where it is writ, Vithaldass Ward, Maruthy Aiyer Ward, I will have a Govindan Nair Ward. My name will thus be writ once in marble. Ah, the mother cat, does one know where she takes us?'

'Which is to say?' I venture.

'Which is to say, your three storeys will go high. Your leaves will have fallen on Shiva. The hunter has to feed his children; the divisional clerk will have to build a house for his august wife. Understood, sir? This is our secret pact,' said Govindan Nair. He went out to spit, and cried back from the veranda: 'I say, it's time for my office'—and jumped across the wall and was gone. What a will-o'-the-wisp of a wall it is, going from nowhere to nowhere; tile-covered, bulging, and obstreperous, it seems like the sound heard and not the word understood. It runs just a little above my window, half an inch higher, and on the other side it dips and rises, running about on its wild, vicarious course. The *bilva* leaves fall on the wall. And sometimes as if to remind us what a serious tree it is, a *bilva* fruit drops over the cowshed on the other side, and the thud makes even the cattle rise. The cattle see me, and urinate. The smell of dung and urine of kine is sweet to me. Purity is so near, so concrete. Let us build the house. Lord, let me build the house.

12

Govindan Nair is a terrible man: huge in his sinews but important in his thought, devious though it is—for it will take you, as some tribespeople do that lead you through jungle and briar, beside the bones of hyena and of panther, and ichor smells of the elephant, and up again through narrow pathways, wind against nostrils, that of a sudden show you his Lord the Tiger might have passed by just now, just a moment ago, look at his paw prints there, and you hear the tiger call while sharp sword-grass is grating your feet; and once up the ledge, standing under a tree, the tribesman will whispering say: 'There, look, that's the Pandya Waterfall, Mother Bhavani's secret trysting place with Lord Shiva,' and you shudder at the beauty and the silence—such are Govindan Nair's twists of passage and of thought which take you through fearful twists and trysts and imponderables, to some majesty. Meanwhile he says his mantra (even while he talks), and you hold your breath. Look, look, there Shiva comes down three days before full moon and in *Marghashira*[4] to

4. The lunar month that falls in December—January..

13

besport himself with his spouse Bhavani. The river therefore carries flowers, and the young tigress cubs. The mother cat, why, haven't you seen it—it walks on any garden wall . . .

Were you certain of the tribesman's mantra, there's still terror in your limbs; you never know where you'll emerge. But were you to land in a ditch, or be transported to another world and to another life, you know that for a moment you've beheld Bhavani as she falls into the sheer silence of the valley, and water foams in frolicsome splendour. Happiness is so simple. You just have to know footpaths. I ask you, does the waterfall ever change?

But sometimes sickness may come, and that's another matter. For that's what happened to me.

That year, the year 1941, you remember the summer came in early. It was hardly February when the heat began to rise, and people wondered where it was all going to end. The grasses grew corrugated, people were afraid cattle fodder would go dearer.

The rice fields were getting baked up. For four months we had no rains. People said of course it's the wars; what is there to be done? You cannot commit such crimes and expect the rains to fall as usual. Man must pay for his sins in slow death. There must be some balance in heaven. When opposites are equalled that is peace. If you kill you get killed, that is the law of nature. Hitler and the British brought about the drought.

Many persons in Trivandrum fell ill with this or that disease. Our Revenue Board Third Member, Kunni Kutta Nair, fell with a thud into his courtyard, and blood came out of his nose. It was diagnosed as one thing, and he died of another. People also died of cholera. Some had, like me, strange boils. It started one morning as I began to scratch my feet. The red of my scratch began to swell up. It became round and then yellow. With difficulty I took my bath and limped to the office. From Puttenchantai, as you know, to the Secretariat is just about twelve minutes' walk. It took me twenty-five but the bubo grew and grew. When my boss suddenly came in around eleven-thirty, asking for some file,

I jumped up, and the bubo burst under my feet. The fluid just spilled over the floor. I gave my boss the file and went into the bathroom (on the way I asked Krishna, the peon, to call the sweeper woman and have the floor cleaned). Once in the bathroom, I found another red spot rising on my thigh. This time there was no question. It almost grew big under my eyes. It was like a guava in a few minutes. But because it gave me no pain, I just went back to my table. In a few hours my whole body except my face had nothing but boils. They rose, grew red and then yellow, añd burst like country eggs. I went to the chemists' and they gave me an ointment and bandages. I walked home with four bandages. I could not touch anything except coffee, I had such disgust. What's the use of having a wife if she cannot take care of one—for when boils come, do they say, Dear Sir, I am coming, may I come, like a mother-in-law? No, they come just like that, and occupy your house. They're of British make, and like everything British, it works without your knowing. Govindan Nair has a simple definition: 'Britain has no secret service—

16

Britain is secret service. Hitler has bombs; the British have boils. But of the two, which one works, dear sir, great sir? Of course the boils.'

Yes, the British boils worked. Some even said the infection was carried back by soldiers from Benghazi. (Where there's no water in the air, the skin swells, avid for any available humidity, is the immediate explanation of Govindan Nair. He has an explanation, as you see, for everything. And every occasion is Serious, intelligible, and final). That night, to come back to my British boils, I was up and hunting my boils as one hunts lice in a girl's hair. I must tell you frankly: I liked it all—just as the girls like lice being killed, there's an acute sense of pleasure when the two nails rub against each other, and the *chit* sound emerges. The louse is well and happily dead. As a child I also liked the sound of lice being killed in my hair. It made you feel life was worth something. So that when the British boils came, I just lay down and counted all of them towards the early morning. There were some forty-four—small and big, red, pink, and white. When they burst I took away the pus, carefully folded it all up in cotton wool, and put it in a corner. When I woke towards morning ants and lizards were both at it. They were having a feast.

I could hardly walk now. When I sat up (for this happened constantly with me, whenever I needed him but never asked for him, there would be Govindan Nair), there he was jumping over the wall. His son Modhu had a cough, and this had kept Govindan Nair awake the whole night; so, as he could not go to sleep, he came for a chat. 'My son will bring my coffee here. Meanwhile let's bark some nonsense.' That's how he always talks.

'Ah,' I said, and showed him the British boils. He looked at the lizards and their feed and said, '*Chee-chee*, get away,' as if they were dogs. For him the whole world was one living organism. Everybody—every thing— understood speech. For him every thing was in masculine gender. He had no verbs in his tongue.

So the British boils came in for close scrutiny. He knew immediately what it was. He knew every thing for he was so concerned with every thing. Once he talked so much on manure that an agricultural expert asked if he was a professor at the local college. Just the same way he talked of the twenty-three types of Enfield guns. Or for that matter of boils. Two cups of coffee were handed down the wall. You just saw hair and hand and Govindan Nair brought in the coffee. The sun was up and the light played on his head. 'Ah, you big British boil,' he said, and laughed.

'Let's drive the British out,' he declared, and after a quarter of an hour's silence— during which he did nothing but play with his toenails—he added: 'And now for the fight.' In half an hour he had been to Narayan Pandita Vaidyan. The medicine smelled disgusting, like horse dung. 'To fight evil you must use evil,' he assured me. I swallowed the paste and fell on the bed exhausted. The Lord knows how much pus must have eked itself out. Shridhar, Govindan Nair's second son, came in again and again, to inquire if Uncle wanted anything.

Then I woke up so long afterward . . . Where was I? The definition of Truth is simple—you wake up and you are in front of Truth.

For when I woke up I thought I saw someone. But actually it was nobody. It was as if Govindan Nair was there when he was not there but yet he was truly there: one can be and not be but be, and where one is one cannot be seen, for light cannot see light and much less can light see the sun.

So when I woke up and, frightened, said: 'Who's there?' I wanted to see something on the chair in front of me. But actually I saw Govindan Nair hiding behind the door. He went to the window (for he was munching tobacco) to spit out and said: 'I am Govindan Nair.' His son Shridhar stood by him brave and well protected. But what had happened in all truth? What, I ask of you?

The facts are there. Shridhar had not been very well, and Narayan Pandita Vaidyan had ordered complete rest, with an oil bath towards noon. So that when Govindan Nair returned for his midday meal (his office was between the Secretariat and the General

Hospital, on the Statue Road—a low-down-looking shed with sacks and a huge red-coloured scale in the middle, and men at the desk examining ration cards—and above was his august office), Shridhar usually woke up, held his father's coat and hung it on the rack. Then he took a towel and held it forth for his father to wipe his feet. Meanwhile his brother Modhu would return. Modhu preferred to eat in the kitchen and to have the meal quickly finished and over—so he could run back to school and have a bout of football. Today, however, he did not return—he had some schoolwork. (At such times he usually ate something in the coffee shop opposite). Shridhar took the towel back to the bathroom and went and lay down on his bed.

Govindan Nair was at his meal, and suddenly he said: 'And, son, what about our delightful neighbour? Is he still emptying his bowels? Has the horse-dung-smelling purge worked?' The son answered: 'Father, I have not been to see him since eleven o'clock, that is, since I started on the oil bath.' 'And you,' Govindan Nair said to his wife, 'and you, my lady, I imagine you are too virtuous to find out whether our friend is living or dead. I fear the medicine was very strong. Ah, our Vaidyans![5] They know how to purge a calf but not a delicate Saraswath Brahmin. Shridhar, go and see.'

It was a very hot day in March. No, it was actually April, getting on to May. The sun was indeed very hot. The *bilva* tree seemed more thorn than leaf, more sun than air. Shridhar, so I learned later, jumped down the garden wall and entered my house from the backyard. He saw me, so he said, lying flat, my face to one side, my latrine bucket gone rolling on itself, and lying handle out in a corner. I was obviously unconscious. Going to the latrine, with the sun so hot, and I so weak, I must have tumbled and fallen against the threshold. I could not reach the bathroom. 'Uncle is dead, Uncle is dead!' shouted Shridhar in terror, running back to the garden wall. Govindan Nair, so I was told, jumped like a three-year-old heifer, washed his hands, and stood

---

5. Doctors who practise the ancient Indian system of medicine, Ayurveda.

beside me. He touched me and felt my pulse. He carried me to my bed. Shridhar fanned me. His mother stood at the wall trying to learn what was happening. Govindan Nair jumped back across the wall. He says nothing more. What did he bring?—The chair was empty. Why are they all in the next room? I wondered. Shridhar suddenly came in, took a fan and started giving me breeze. From the window I could see Tangamma handing a tumbler of coffee—so hot, she had a towel around it—to Govindan Nair. 'Sir, here is your nectar,' he said. 'Everybody has his nectar. Mine is tobacco juice, and yours the juice of a blackberry. At the ration department we are told we live on thirty ounces of rice per person. I solemnly declare, we live on nectar. Man does not live on terrestrial viands. He lives on the fruits of heaven.' And he laughed as he propped me up in bed and, holding me with one hand, gave me coffee with the other. Shridhar was still fanning. Tangamma was standing by the wall playing with a trefoil of *bilva*. Where was I? Where was my wife? Does *bilva* make nectar, I wondered. I must ask Narayan Pandita Vaidyan. Suddenly I had to go to the latrine again. 'The bowels are a tremendous responsibility of man, three hundred miles of guts hold a few handfuls of chemical compost. And this little chemical mixture makes or unmakes the stability of man. Funny, isn't it?' Govindan Nair said this, and stood by the door to the courtyard. 'Call me, brother, when you want water. Water is our best protector against sin. To smell is sin. To do is no sin. To gulp is sin. To purge is bounty. To die is fanciful. Reality is when you die really. Shridhar's death is my joke. When you fall unconscious they say you are dead. In fact where were you, brother, when Shridhar thought you were dead? Were you dead to yourself, my friend? You purge to live. You sleep to die. When sleep is life, where is death? Ha, ha, ha,' he laughed, keeping me company from outside, while my bowels were pouring down hot liquid. I thought my guts would come out. There's such innocence in a purged body. Disease is unnatural. Death is natural. To die rightly is to wake and find one has ever been being.

Shridhar knew his father as he knew his textbook. (He always stood second or third in class. He was in the fourth form.) A cigarette was bought from the neighbouring shop, and a matchbox. Sitting by the window, Govindan Nair lit his cigarette, while Shridhar returned to give back the matchbox to the shopkeeper—then, coming back, he started fanning me again. I said, 'I must build a house of three storeys anyway. My wife can hire out the first two floors if need be. It will be so much capital invested. A house of three storeys these days is a safe investment. How much would it cost? One can live on the third floor.'

'Thirty thousand rupees, if there's no inflation after the war,' Govindan Nair declared. 'Let's begin buying this house, for the moment. A bird in hand is worth two in the bush. Govindan Nair in Trivandrum is worth two wives in Kartikura House. Isn't that so, brother?' he said, but looking towards the wall, he saw Tangamma hide her mouth with the palm of her hand, and laugh.

I have developed a bad habit. I like women. Not that I like all sorts of women. I like woman, in fact. What is woman, you may ask. Well, woman is Shantha. Shantha is a school teacher in the Nair Society High School. She is fairly tall, and has delicate hands. I am not particularly tall or fair or good or bad. I am just a man. And Shantha is not just a woman, she is woman. I think often of the child she will bear forth (that is, when he will appear), and I cry with delight even before the time is come. Shantha lives with her mother and two brothers round near the Poolimood. The brothers go to school. The mother cooks. Shantha earns (they have some property too, in north Travancore). Shantha also loves. Her house is not far. Only in monsoon are the roads very difficult. Even so we somehow manage to be with each other. I can cough just a little, then Shantha will put her pillow against my neck. That is why she is so exquisite in her love play. She is shy like a peahen. Her giving is complete. But the truth is, who is there to take? Can you? There's a story said of Sinbad the sailor. He was told by the jinn: Take, take all the royal treasury. He opened his hands to take. The hands had changed into gold. (I read this in my old school text).

That's taking. Saroja of Kartikura House is a true Brahmin. She knows how to take. But Shantha is a Nair. Nairs worship their mothers and recognize their fathers. I liked my father and had affection for my mother. The world has to be worshipped. Shantha worships me and has herself. I worship nothing (no, not even money, although it will make the three storeys possible), and I don't think I care for anything. Caring for nothing is to use everything for oneself. Caring for oneself is to give things their self. Shantha loves me, and so she will have a beautiful boy. She's not worried about marriage. I am a Brahmin. Shantha is not ashamed to be woman. I am afraid to be a man.

That is why I carry Shantha so badly on my face. When Govindan Nair wants to speak of her, he simply says, the Vazhavan-kad house (Vazhavan is a small hamlet in north Travancore). He calls her by her house name as if her house were she. In fact her house is she. To speak the truth, that is how I met her. She came to the Revenue Board about some land division. She looked so innocent, I told her to sit down and immediately took out her file. She was sure her case was right for she could not know how her face might ever be wrong. Might she think of anything wrong? She was certain she could not. So truth became her thought. If she said, 'Come to me'—it meant come. If she became my mistress it was because she felt wife. She remained a wife. My feet were there for her to worship. My weaknesses were there for her to learn; my manhood, at least such as I possess, for her to bear children. She had never touched any man before. She said she knew me to be her man the moment I went and stood against the filing ladder. For a woman love is not development. Love is recognition. The fact that my intestinal troubles improved after I met her proved she was right, so she felt. Devotion to me was proof of her truth. The child was meaning. The woman is always right.

Who told Shantha then that I had fallen unconscious? She said my son (in her) told her so. She went to Govindan Nair's house, and she and Tangamma stood at the wall, while Shridhar came to open my window. Shantha would never come to me. How could she come to my wife's house? She looked from under the *bilva* tree, her figure square and big, and I could see tears fall from her eyes. She seemed to be more in prayer than in sorrow; her skin shone like black ivory, so it had the colour of blue. I could almost (I used to tease her) see the white hands of the child inside of her (for I am sort of Brahmin-fair). Will this illness affect the child? I must build a house, a house three storeys high.

Destiny brings to us little slips of paper, as the office peon does from some visitor or the boss. What does a name really mean? The British bubo is a name given by my friend Govindan Nair to an unknown phenomenon of physiological eruption, when pus and blood seem to rise on the skin, round themselves up like a country mango, and split, and the flies and the lizards have the feast. Now that the bubos are finished, tell me, who will feast the lizards? Who will feed the bacilli, if indeed it was a bacillus and it came from Benghazi? Is it really so hot in Benghazi? What made some autonomous invisible crawly active entity enter into an Indian soldier in his wars with Hitler and Rommel, burst into a million bloody worms which having travelled through boats, trains, restaurants (through the files of the sanitary inspectors' reports), penetrate into some flies perchance that sat on a cow whose milk my milkman brings, and, having gone into my intestines where the bacilli field was relatively vacant (like an empty conference room, chairs and tables set out and the meeting might begin at any time and the resolution be passed), give me, sir dear sir, my beautiful British bubo? Everybody must do something—the clerk must correct his files, the fleas must bite. Illness come, and one goes to Narayan Pandita Vaidyan, and the horse-dung medicine is given. I go for the purge, the sun is hot, I tumble against the threshold and fall. And that's Shridhar's death. For him an unconscious state is death. What is sleep then to Shridhar?

Poor Shridhar was also ill. He had malaria (or was it filaria?)—another flea bite. So he did not go to school. One goes to school when one is well (and when Uncle is not ill). Thus the two flea families had made a pact. Across the wall they said to each other: 'We will change the world. You come from Benghazi and I come from, say, Uzhavezhapuram. We met and we shall play destiny.' Invisible are the ways of destiny. Food will go across the wall—Shridhar will not go to school. 'Pappadam and rice will I take down to Uncle.' The *bilva* tree will bless.

Shantha is carrying four months. I can just see the rise in her belly, from where I lie. Her smile is freedom of the world. It is trust in herself. She looks in as I look out (as Shridhar does). To trust is to be. She can lean against the wall whispering out words to me, as if the world would create itself to her wishes for me. She created a child for herself and gave it to me. She said, 'This is yours.' And that is the truth. Who can create a child but God . . . What is the relation between God and Shantha?

'I go and come.' Shantha smiles from the wall. She, as it were, bows to me behind her back. Then slowly I hear the leaves of the jack trees crunch under her. I now see the head first, blue as sky, then the hair (with flat big chignon), and then she is gone. For a long time I go on listening to myself like a lizard. It is beginning to be hot already. Tangamma sends Shridhar with some coffee to console me. Then Govindan Nair (with sandal paste on his forehead and his packet of betel leaves and tobacco) jumps across the wall.

'How are you, my lord and liege?'

'Better than if the kingdom were at peace and no wars anywhere.'

'The Hitlers are in us, like objects in seeing. We think there is Hitler, when Hitler is really an incarnation of what I think. You are bad because I am. You are good because I am. The sun is because I see. You do not suffer because you are the British bubo. Ah, brother, you too be British'—and he guffawed. He liked his own jokes, and tears came to his eyes. Then he smiled in love. 'I love the British. I respect them because they are such shopkeepers. What can you do after all? If you have to buy you must sell. If you want betel and tobacco, you must work in numbers. You issue ration cards, six hundred seventy a day, and God gives food to the needful. I must say I have never come across so much respect for God as amongst the British. I often think God is a ledger keeper. Loss and gain do not interest him. Accounts do. Even a rat can give trouble to the British.'

'How so?' I ask. Govindan Nair's methods are so devious. I just do not understand.

'Rats eat up accounts. That is how we explained away the ration given to Kolliathur village. When the big boss asked, 'Where are the files?' we made such a grand search. First my boss said: 'We have misplaced it.' Then he said: 'We do not think we have it in this office.' Finally he wrote: 'Eaten away by rats. Please ask the Public Works Dept. Officer to come to Ration Office No. 66 for inspection. Two reports on rat pest remain unanswered.'

'What happened then?'

'He built a house, that is John did. He built a modest little house. He said it was done from the proceeds of his wife's property sale. Her grandmother had just died. Everybody has a grandmother, you know.'

'Where is the house?'

'On the Karamanai side.'

'Is it expensive?'

33

'Only some fifteen thousand rupees. The Brahmins are getting poorer with the wars. So they sell their houses. Why, soldiers earn more than clerks today. That is the law of the rats.'

'What do you do then for the rats?'

'We encourage them. We even invite them, like the Pied Piper, with music.'

'Seriously speaking?'

'Dead seriously. Rats are necessary for the ration shops. Otherwise who will eat up all the rice? If you want the population of Trivandrum to feed on food, then you have to employ other means.'

'What?' I asked in my denseness.

'Ah, sir, you need the mother cat,' he said in utter gravity, then rose and spat out tobacco.

'Shridhar!' he shouted. 'Bring two cups of coffee.' And settling down, he put some more chalk to his betel, and started chewing again.

'You need education, sir. You are poor in general knowledge. You do not know you have a grandmother. You know too little about rats. You must become a pathologist and write a paper on the nature of bacteria, as seen in ration-shop ledgers. One rich man in the north, so I heard, was travelling on a train. Where are you going, Seth Sahib? they asked him. I'm going to Jagannath Puri, sirs, for the annual festival of the Lord of Earth. Why, do you belong hereabouts? they said. No, sirs, I come from Calcutta. I am a grain merchant, he said. The famine, we hear is very serious now, they said. Yes sirs, who should know it but me? he said. It must be terrible, they said. Yes, I am going to Jagannath Puri. I am giving the Lord a silver spire, the grain merchant said. Now, I ask of you, my friend, when shall we build your golden spire?'

'When do you want to?'

'In four or five months Shantha will have an heir. Let us build a spire ten men high.'

'It will be three storeys high.'

'First let us build one two storeys high.'

'Anything you like,' I said, laughing.

'No sir, it is a dead serious matter. A woman bears a child. The child needs a basic house to be born in. You cannot be born just anywhere. Let us buy this house itself,' he said, spitting out his tobacco. Shridhar had brought in the coffee. He stood there, amazed and in admiration before his father. His father looked like a sea captain hatching plans to decoy a cargo. The night is falling. The sea is calm. The sea will obey the captain. 'Captain, the sea of Arabia is mild.' 'Turn towards the Laccadive Archipelago.' 'The Dutch ships sail.' 'Who cares if they have guns? We have sinews. You build empires. We build houses. Slaves, to the nor'east!'

One must build a house if one has to have a house, I say to myself. We'll plant a *bilva* tree by it. Shantha will look at me, whispering words. How beautiful it is to be pregnant. Why not always be pregnant and four months carrying? You can play with *bilva* leaves, and, like the hunter, you can go on dropping them on the silence below. Shiva will appear. I envy women that they bear children.

'Usha will be coming back from school,' I sit and say, as if to the chair. I have a canvas chair, and, my feet on its edge, I scratch the curve of my limbs, and I think. The coffee has just gone down my throat. I have been to the Home Friends to have my bad cup of coffee. (Sometimes I want to avoid this, and go to the milk bar near my office and gulp a cup of milk. I feel so virtuous after that. But milk is never an immediate friend like coffee. In life we search for truth but live in the illusion of permanence. Milk is good for me. 'It is good for the mother cat,' Govindan will shout, and laugh, 'No cat will ever touch your potion of the dark bean. We have no feline instinct. We live like rats,' etc., etc.) Thinking of Usha of an evening is a pleasant thing. I could always take her out on a walk: 'Come, child,' and she will leave her book and give her little finger for me to take. And so we go. Usha is the dearest thing in my life. She is my child. She is not merely that. She is child. When I hear somebody say, he walks, you may think it is an impersonal, a grammatically correct statement. I walk, he walks, they walk. But for me walking is Usha. When she sits it is sitting. Shantha understands this. Shantha's silence has all that logic cannot compute. Saroja wants two and two to make four, and if I say, 'What about your dreams, there do two and two make four?' she says, 'It always makes four, according to me. Yet in the logic of my dreams it's seven. But I am not living in a dream. Usha is five years old. She is not ten. You can open the school register and see.'

When you have Saroja's logic, what can you do? What logic, Usha must ask herself, has the railway train that says Kimkoo-chig, chug, chug, as if it were a great-aunt, and it goes on spitting out fire at the Elayathur railway station? The train watches all school returners. Evening after evening it will come and spit out friendly smoke. The cigarette vendors, the *wada* sellers, the coolies, the *jhatka-* and *bandi-walas*[6] outside will all have a logic with the train system. Soon after the train arrives, passengers will get out. They have so many bundles. Usha is sure the train knows it. She knows too that *jhatkas* come in the right numbers. As there are so many benches at the school every morning for so

6. *Jhatka* is a horse carriage and a *bandi* is a cart drawn by bullocks.

many children, you have so many *jhatkas*. Every evening you have so many *bandis*. Snakes know when the school children pass. The train has told them: Take care, take care, they are under my protection.

I love Usha for the way she comes back from school. She dreams of the train behind her. She has no fear. For the train will let her pass first on the Sethupallea bridge. Then you go down and stand in the field below, under the small young coconut tree. The train is happy. The tree says, 'Good morning,' as the soldiers say to one another. Usha and her friends put stones around the tree. They are building a marriage house. Once the train has passed with all the men and women, faces and shouts, Usha feels she can go home. Saroja does not wait for her. She is busy inspecting the rope making. Saroja is a tremendous worker. For her fact is that which yields. Her fathers have left thirty-three acres of wet land. They worked hard. They gave her and her sister education. Land is a fact. You reap what you sow.

I have a system of no logic, and that is the story. What logic can speak of Usha?

How and what shall I say about Shantha? She lives backwards, as it were, when, with her rounded belly, she moves forward. Birth is instantaneous with time. Who is born where? Time is born in time. And that is Shantha. To be a wife is not to be wed. To be a wife is to worship your man. Then you are born. And you give birth to what is born in being born. You annihilate time and you become a wife. Wifehood, of all states in the world, seems the most holy. It stops work. It creates. It lives on even when time dies. Suppose you broke your clock, would the garden go? Suppose the garden were burned, where will the sky go? Such is woman.

I was thinking of the house and of Usha, scratching my feet, sitting on the canvas chair. The evening will slowly draw in bringing the sea nearer. How the night coming gives trees and sound a peculiar shy truth. They want to hide and go and come. Morning will reveal them, as if they had gone somewhere, and returned. The *bilva* tree always seems on a voyage to nowhere. It has gone and come like a clock that ticks. Time ticks. You close your eyes and open. I want to be free.

Shall I build a house for Usha? Who will give the money? I ask myself. Shantha could if she wished. My office can have her papers registered, and she could then have her disputed land, and she can sell it. Shantha loves Usha without having seen her. Shantha's house will be the right house for Usha. Vithal my son will inherit from his mother . . .

'Don't worry, brother,' says Govindan Nair, coming in after his bath. He has *The Hindu* in his hand. The newspaper is visible truth, is one of his theories. When truth becomes visible, it is a life. So the world is a life, etc., etc.

'As true as *The Hindu*, I tell you I will help you to build the house.'

'With what?' I ask.

'With bricks,' he says, and roars in laughter. 'A house, dear sir, is built with bricks. In dreams you can build it in gold. In the Mahabharata you build it in lacquer. I will build it for you in stone.'

'But stone will make it hot.'

'Stone gives permanence to objects. You must have a house that will last five hundred years. Someone in history will say: This house of stone, in the ruins of old Trivandrum, is one thousand one hundred years old. Look at its inscriptions. They are in Roman characters. That was the character used universally for some five hundred years. It was called the period of the big empires. They set. The Indians quarrelled among themselves. Then the Huns came. We fought the Huns. Some soldiers scratching the wall found a name. It read: Govindan Nair, Ration Clerk. They thought it meant a general. Or a prince. He who gives is a prince. I give rations or rather ration cards, so I give food. I am a prince, we will therefore build a palace. The palace of truth.'

I never could understand all that he meant. He always seemed to be pulling my leg. 'Yes, sir, the cat always meows. That is my nature, to say meow-meow. All my language can be reduced to that—meow, meow, meowooow.'

I love Govindan Nair.

Hearing I was ill, Saroja brought Usha by the morning train. It comes in at ten-ten and she left by the evening local at four forty-

42

three. She had boat repairs to inspect—boats had to carry away coconut shells. Her land is in the Elayathur lagoon. A patch of land surrounded by water. There are such deep-bent coconut trees. And you hear the sea.

Shantha said to me one evening: 'When my land is sold, we'll buy this house,' by which she meant my house. She never came inside, but it was *this* house for it was mine. That is the way with woman. What belongs to you belongs to me, what belongs to the lord alone belongs. For woman is belonging, as mind is belonging—belonging to me. You can only shine of light. The shine knows its light, but to whom does the light belong? Light belongs to light. Lord, how beautiful thou hast made woman! She *tells* you. If woman were not, would you know you were? Shantha said: 'You,' and I saw I. Wonderful is man. He needs to be told he is. Then he knows he is. Looking alone he sees himself and tries to say: You. He is dumb. He cannot speak. He makes a bare movement of lips. The mirror says so. There is no sound. But sound comes and tells him: 'You.' Who said 'You?' She. Thus the world goes moving on its pivot.

Usha goes along the railway line. The railway engine is kind to her. When the wind blows in gusts, and the monsoon comes pouring through the coconut trees, the train blows and blows the whistle, and says: 'Child, child, I am coming. Please keep away from the railway line. I am your mother. I protect you, even though you see me come and go. I dream of you in my roundhouse. In the Trivandrum roundhouse there are many old hags. They were all made in foundries before this era was born. But I was born in 1921. I have grown up among coconut trees. I have played with the Kanchi and Kali rivers. I know every bridge by its sound. I whistle past Kartikura House. I know the sound of my whistle wakes up the wildcats on your roof. They have such bright eyes. I come to protect. I am the thread of your lives. What would you do without the railway line? How will you go to school otherwise? The signal is my eldest daughter, the shunting hand my granddaughter. Children, children, who go to school, keep away from the railway line: I am passing.' And the engine floods the line with milky light.

Man is protected. You could not be without a mother. You are always a child. The wife is she who makes you the child. That is why our children resemble us men.

And no sooner is the mind made up, than the hand does. For one morning—or was it evening?—it must have been evening, for I could see him with his body bare down to the waist, fresh with a cool bath, a cigarette in his hand (he would not smoke before his morning meal), Govindan Nair came to see me. Fat in his big presence, he stood at the door not wanting to disturb me with his smoke. I adjusted my glasses and looked up. (I must have been at my *Malayalarajyam*. I was away in the Hitler wars and Churchill communiques.)

He said: 'Sir, it's done.'

I said: 'What?'

'I say, sir, it is done. The thing is done. You have it when you want.' I think I understood. But I was not sure. I was afraid to know lest the knowing be false. So I said: 'Which?'

He said: 'That.'

I was dumbfounded. 'And that is?'

'That is this,' he said as if he had said everything. He loved, because of his big heart, to say obvious things in parables, and make you think it was all such a small affair. He was like Bhima.[7] You want the flower of paradise? Why, here I go and come. And Hanuman himself will help, Hanuman his half-brother, unknown unto Bhima. Everybody is half-brother to you, man and thing. So why worry? That seemed the principle on which Govindan Nair worked: I am, so you are my brother.

'It's done.' And he placed the book in front of me. It was covered with yellowed newspaper. It looked like a school exercise book. He had copied *Astavakra Samhita*,[8] and he often carried it with him. He liked to recite '*Aho Aham Namo Mahyam Yasyame Nastikinchana.*'[9] He opened the book and started reading it out to me in beautiful

---

7. A well-known story in a dance drama. Bhima, a hero of the Mahabharata, is helped by Hanuman, a figure in the Ramayana, to find the flower of paradise.

8. A famous text on pure Vedanta.

9. 'Wonderful am I! Adoration to myself who love nothing.'

Sanskrit. Though a Brahmin I knew less Sanskrit than he. And I understood even less. He recited verse after verse. (Shridhar brought us our coffee.) He read several chapters right through as if they said what he wanted to say. Then abruptly he closed the book with his left hand and started looking at the newspaper. He liked politics. He admired courage. He always loved people who went in search of the paradise flower. It meant you became half-brother to mankind. Govindan Nair loved slipping in two rupees and five rupees through windows where a child cried. He thought his intentions would help. Fortunately his wife had lands, and the rice came in plentifully. Otherwise, how to live on forty-five rupees a month, a second clerk in Ration Office No. 66? Or buy houses, you understand.

Life is a riddle that can be solved with a riddle. You can remove a thorn with another thorn, you solve one problem through another problem. Thus the world is connected. The ration shop is meant to fight famine, and famine is there because there is war, and war because of the British, and the British because of whom? Danes, Normans, etc., say the textbooks. But actually who cares? If you fight the British in the ration shop, you solve the British problem. If you have the British bubo, you take the horse-dung medicine of Narayan Pandita Vaidyan. You get a disease from Benghazi and Narayan Pandita Vaidyan cures this unknown. The unknown alone resolves the unknown. So, brother, work and be merry, distribute cards in Ration Office No. 66. 'Shridhar, go and tell your mother my friend is languishing because he has no strength in his limbs. His flower of paradise is coffee bean. When it is burned black and its powder is made into a collation, its effect on limbs and mind is excellent, for intellect and heart. Sir, let us go on to our *Astavakra*.'

Govindan Nair sat on the veranda of my house. He forgot his food. My stomach was bubbling with demand. Fortunately the coffee had come in once again. Till nine o'clock, he read the *Astavakra Samhita* from any where to the very end, and then he said: 'I have done a good job. I have explained to the Brahmin what Brahman is. "Brahmin is he who knows Brahman," etc., etc. Ruling princes taught sadhus the Truth in the Upanishadic times. Now Nairs alone can teach the Truth in the world.' I knew at once he was right. He was right. He is right. He will ever be right.

'Isn't it time to be coming home?' whispered Tangamma from the wall. 'The children have gone to sleep.'

'Good night, sir,' he said as if he had said what he wanted to say to me, and jumped across the wall—there was such flowing moonlight on the *bilva* tree. I walked thoughtfully along the road to the Home Friends. Would they still have chapattis. A hungry stomach is a bad friend. It smells bad. There were chapattis, Ananthkrishnan said, and I felt good.

Ration Office No. 66 is just above Ration Shop No. 181. As I told you, it is on Statue Road, between the Secretariat and the General Hospital, beside the mansion of Justice Varadaraj Iyengar (the man known in Trivandrum for having hanged more people in his lifetime than any other living magistrate. For him evil was concrete, and he had it removed from the mass of mankind. So he gave the best punishment. 'It makes our daughters hope for better marriages,' he said. And it did). Varadaraj Iyengar, of course, as everybody knows, finally died, and he died far away and well, in some Himalayan hermitage he had constructed overlooking the young Ganges. Nobody did him any harm. People knew he was just. He lived like a hermit, with but one family servant, and he died peacefully reciting some mantra. His ashes were flown to Benares. Thus he died a happy man.

Just next to this mansion, almost touching his casuarina tree at the door, is Ration Shop No. 181. It is an old garage of Mr Shiva Shankra Pillai, the retired Tahsildar, who himself married from Mavelikara, that is from just where Her Highness the Maharani comes. Shiva Shankra Pillai had two sons and both of them turned bad. One enlisted and went to the wars a subaltern. The other opened a cloth shop at Chalai, and is doing good business. The daughter married well; she is the daughter-in-law of Kunni Krishna

Menon and she lives happily. All that is old is stable. Otherwise how could you say it is stable? It is stable because it is traditional. So Kunni Krishna Menon, with huge estates run well, continued the tradition of his ancestors. He and his wife amassed a fortune—thus Shiva Shankra Pillai's daughter was happy. Her children often came to see their grandfather and usually went through the ration shop up to the ration office. The garage had drivers' quarters at the top. This and the garage were extended so that the ration shop and office ran all over the pentagonal shapes, with four rooms at the top and five at the bottom.

The children liked to play among the chillies and tamarind, for these were sold as a side line by the ration-shop vendor to make a little extra money. His programme was, he who eats rice cannot eat it alone, so why not make some more profit? Government or no government, who is there to come and see? Sometimes the children went and sat in the huge scales, shouting and chaffing, one weighing against the other till the women, who came with their baskets and sacks, would jerk and let the scale go from one side to the other as if it were a cradle. And the louder shouted the children, the wilder became the crowd. Meanwhile people from the street came rushing forward to see the fun, and old ladies standing in the queue would say: 'The sun is hot for us. The fun is over now. Why make us hunger more?' And from the staircase of the ration office, a head or two would show, to prove that under the office is the ration shop, and one should not play with such serious things. What is this nonsense going on? The first to come would of course be Govindan Nair, his underclothes showing (it was always too hot for him) and a pen in his hand. He had a long nose, pointed and expressive, and when he turned anywhere, it was as if he could speak with his nose. He looked at the children and laughed. Then, going to the scale, he pushed the needle to the middle and said: 'Everything in the world weighs the same. Look, look!' And the women looked up and saw and said: 'Of course, look, everybody weighs the same. How did he do it?' The children lost some fun. But when he let go, he did so with a bump, and the younger child went up shouting: 'Father!

Father!' Then he caught hold of one of the children of the crowd and set it against the uplifted child. The scale went down with a thud. The elder child, called Gopi, cried. 'Gopi, Gopi,' said Govindan Nair, 'you can't always be at the top. Even Hitler some time has to come down. Now, children, you go home to grandpapa. When you come next time I'll build you a swing in the garden. And I will sit with you under the casuarina tree. And we shall see the sky.' Meanwhile, half of the ration office staff—except, of course, the boss, Bhoothalinga Iyer (he lived in the fort near the temple, an honest, disgruntled man with a hair knot on his head, *namam*[10] on his face, and a Ramayana on his lap; so he sat, looking after the ration office)—would come down.

There are very few interesting faces in the ration office. Abraham is a Syrian Christian from Nagercoil, and he looks the very image of Christ with his flat face and longish beard. He hurts no one, he earns enough for his childless wife and himself, and he smokes

---

10. Sacred marks.

incessantly. Sometimes he talks poetry to Govindan Nair, especially of Eletchan,[11] and they compare notes on Malayalam words. When everything is over, Govindan Nair will say: 'Man, how can you know Malayalam? You have to be a Nair.' Abraham accepted this as an axiom. Only a Nair can know Malayalam. Only a Nair can belong to Malabar. Only a Nair can see right. Look at the boss, Bhoothalinga Iyer. He can no more understand truth than the buffalo can see a straight line.

Velayudhan Nair is the opposite number of Govindan Nair. He is tall and fair and shouts at the top of his voice that his father was a Brahmin. That does not make him equal either to Bhoothalinga Iyer or to Govindan Nair. He is one with one and other with the other. He manipulates ration cards with a facility that makes everybody wonder whether he learned street jugglery.

There was the famous case of Ration Card No. 65477919, which just disappeared from the office. The register marked the

11. Eletchan wrote the famous Ramayana in Malayalam.

name Appan Pillai, of Medi Vithu, Palayam. The thumb impression of Appan Pillai was there. His people said they have been getting the right rations, but when asked about the card, they said they never received it. Inquiries brought forward four or five such cases. Govindan Nair just joked. He knew A from B as he knew left eye from right eye. He knew just enough about the matter to show Velayudhan Nair he knew. So Velayudhan Nair smiled at him and thought his colleague too would know what was to be known and perform what was to be performed. After all, sir, it is wartime and everybody has children. Two is the limit—but then if you have three—on forty-seven rupees, how can you feed a third child? Especially if it has a bit of difficulty in the spleen? Three years old and she has the belly of one of eight. Spleen may be just a pouch on the left side of man but it gives infinite trouble. It makes the child bloat and cry. What can you do with a child's cry? Doctors are expensive— even government doctors. They don't take fees, but they like gifts. What is the gift for a good-sized spleen? Thirty rupees, etc., etc.

Velayudhan Nair's wife, when you see her at a cinema, has an array of gold bangles on her hands. She inherited some money from her aunt. We all have aunts; why don't we inherit? is a pertinent question and Govindan Nair, who is pertinence itself, asked it. He was interested in children, in houses for children, in medicines for spleen that bloats, etc. When one is curious one can know anything. It's like the kitten seeking the cat, etc. (I use etc. because that is exactly Govindan Nair's language. It comes from working in offices disinterestedly, he says, does Govindan Nair.)

So, to use his phrase, the cat came out of the bag. It was a big cat and the bag was a gunnysack. It smelled peculiarly of rice. There's a saying of Kabir they often quoted in the ration shop: On each grain of rice is writ the name of he who'll eat it. The ration card is the proof. Medicine for spleen is proof of the ration card. The child is proof of his father, said Velayudhan Nair, showing his child to Govindan Nair. 'My son has no spleen. He has malaria or filaria, I don't know what it is,' said Govindan Nair. 'You must take him to a decent doctor,' said Velayudhan Nair. 'Who is your doctor?' asked Govindan Nair. 'Why, Doctor Velu Pillai, MBBS, MRCP from Edinburgh. Specialist in children's diseases.' 'My son is seven years old. He is neither a child nor a man. So where shall we take him?' laughed Govindan Nair. 'Why,' replied Velayudhan Nair, 'I have just the fellow for that. You come here tomorrow at five. And we'll settle it.'

'Ah, sir, the cat is out of the bag,' he said, coming to see me that evening. Hitler was winning his wars. The prices went up. The British army poured into India. India sent rice to Persia. Russia attacked the German left flank. Von Boch was hurtling towards Moscow. Von Rundstedt's armies rushed towards Kiev. The Dnieper Dam was blasted. Paris decreed against Jews. Roosevelt was wiping his spectacles—that was one of the pictures stuck against the wall in our office. We liked Roosevelt because we hated Churchill. We love what we cannot have. When we have it, we have it not, because what it is not, is what we want, and thus on to the wall. The mother cat alone knows. It takes you by the skin of your neck, and takes you to the loft. It alone loves. Sir, do you know love? O Lord, I want to love. I want to love all mankind. Why should there be spleen when in fact there is no malaria? Why don't children sit in scales and play the game of ration cards? Who plays, Lord, who plays? 'Give unto me love that I love,' such was the prayer that went up from across my garden wall to the nowhere.

'How is Shantha?' asked Govindan Nair abruptly, as if suddenly he had seen the mother cat with the kitten, and I said: 'She was asking your wife about a good maternity doctor. Dr Krishna Veni Amma is no good. She is too young. Do you know of one?'

'Yes,' he said. 'I am seeing a child's doctor tomorrow. I think he will do.'

What is a doctor? One who knows diseases is the simplest definition. One who knows a wound and heals a pain is a doctor.

Five o'clock on any watch (including the clock on the Secretariat) is the same moment all over the world. But not the same hour, for the world is regulated by the watch. Pray, what is a watch? A thing that turns on itself and shows the moon. What is the moon? The thing that turns on itself and (elliptically) goes around the sun. And what is the sun? The sun is a luminary that made the earth—the grasses rise green on the sward; the clouds form; the dawn comes; the cattle go home; man puts manhood into woman and the child is born; the tree shoots into the air, and birds sit on it; houses rise, houses, and our children, when they are born, are well looked after . . . Eagles circle. That is all due to the sun. And the moon. And the clock on the Secretariat. (If the government did not run, then who would pay whose debt?) So, at five-fifteen, Velayudhan Nair went over to the table of Govindan Nair (and what an ocean of ration cards was there, with cigarette butts, shirt buttons, broom grass for cleaning the ears, sandal paste—on little banana leaves—dry flowers, books—Eletchan and one or two books on Vedanta—and in the drawers would be pencils, razor blades, stitching needles, and pice. To buy a cigarette the pice is easier to give than an anna. Copper makes the waste simpler, and the boss does not mind it as long as it is cheap and he knows you are not making money on ration cards. Two rupees a ration card is the official black-market price, if you want to know. If you have children you can have ten cards. To have ten children is permitted by law. And the doctors have no objection. 'So we have ten children. Look how well fed I look. My wife has a ruby earring. Look, look at her,' etc., etc.).

Velayudhan Nair says: 'Man, we go to the doctor.' Velayudhan Nair always began every sentence with Man, for he had been to Bombay. In Colaba every De Souza says: Man. This they learned from the P & O ships. And P & O ships touch Plymouth. Do they say 'Man' there, one wonders.

'So, man, we go to the doctor,' he repeated.

'Mr Man, I come,' said Govindan Nair. He sometimes used Mister to show he too could be elegant. He called his son Mr Shridhar. ('Mr Shridhar, go and get me a chew,' 'Mr Shridhar, the thing that father puffs is wanted,' etc., etc. Mr Shridhar therefore brought the chew tobacco or that which father puffs, according to orders.)

Velayudhan Nair: 'Man, it is hot.'

Govindan Nair: 'Mister, it cannot be cold in April.'

Velayudhan Nair (wiping his face): 'Yes, but we will have to wait at the doctor's.'

Govindan Nair: 'Why, is he such a busy man?'

Velayudhan Nair: 'Busy? He is as busy as he wants to be.'

So we go, said Velayudhan Nair, and Govindan Nair pulled the shirt over his body and there they were going to the doctor. The doctor lived off the main road, before you come to the temple. You know, as you go down after the railway bridge, there are a number of cloth shops. Then if you turn to the right—the first lane after where the policeman stands—you come to a small square.

A pleasant rain began to fall. It was refreshing, this cool shower of the heavens. They went up an ordinary tier of house steps, knocked at a much-knobbed door (more like houses in Madras than here), and they entered. It was a living house, obviously, for there was a bronze swing at the far end of the corridor, in the huge hall, where there were many lights. Perhaps the clouds had made the house dark. Suddenly the sun shone and the lights went off. There were many ladies inside the house. There were also some men.

'The doctor is a busy man. Let me go and see,' said Velayudhan Nair, and went towards the swing.

Govindan Nair sat on a sofa and started reading the *Cheeranjivi*.

Nothing is pleasanter than a doctor's waiting room. You have the pleasantest thoughts because you know the doctor will say: 'You have no disease. This is not pneumonia. This is a bad cold. This is not venereal, this is only the British bubo,' etc.

Before you had time to say Rama Krishna, there he was, Velayudhan Nair. They both entered a huge room, opening on the back yard where a lonely neem tree stood. There were many soldiers there, their hands tattooed; there were government officials in slick clothes; there were merchants and even some Communist leaders (who had just been let out of jail). There were bottles on the table.

You could hear women's voices from the other side of the corridor. How they shrieked or hissed, or you heard them sing. One or two of them came out in high-heeled shoes. Some were smoking and even speaking English. A girl came in—an Anglo-Indian no doubt—and spoke in Tommies' tongue. The men who came out were adjusting their clothes and pulling their ties, and laughing. Some of them had their hands on their hair, quite thoughtful. Life looked gay and remote and not altogether comfortable. Life is like that. Life is a ration shop. The scale weighs everything according to the ration card. Where is your ration card, Sir? Green, red, or blue?

Girls were obviously gathered at the back of the big room opposite. 'This is Shiv Shanker Pillai,' muttered Velayudhan Nair, introducing a sleek middle-aged man with an ochre shirt, a clean white elegant dhoti, gold-rimmed glasses—and to speak truly, a gentle, sweet-looking man. 'He is in charge of the clinic,' said Velayudhan Nair, and started smiling as if to himself.

'If the patient could come in and choose his doctor, it would be nice. Like they say in America they have different doctors for different diseases, we have different cures for different horoscopes as it were, and diagnosed by experts. But let us go in.'

Shiv Shanker Pillai opened a big door and Govindan Nair walked in. A large bed lay between the corner and the window to the right. There was also an office table and a chair. A gentle light fell on everything. Even pencil and paper were laid out on the table as if on purpose. 'We write love letters here,' Shiv Shanker Pillai joked. A girl came in from behind them, round, with nose ring and necklace, with black hair and a rich bosom. She was shy. 'The patient may undress while the doctor is getting ready,' said Shiv Shanker Pillai, and went out. He seemed serious in saying this.

The rich bosom heaved. The *choli* came open. The girl started cooing and singing. She danced a mellow dance. Govindan Nair sat on the chair and looked at this with fascination. 'What a beautiful woman you are,' he said. 'Beauty is the core of music.' And she continued to dance. Govindan Nair did not get up. He drew the chair nearer as if to see more clearly. He said again and again, 'You are beautiful, I can see.' Then she stripped herself and lay on the bed. The gold necklace fell so curvedly about her breast. Her shape was comely, a little fat above the down of the belly. She had much pubic hair, he observed. So she did not shave those parts.

'How many children do you have?' asked Govindan Nair.

'Two,' said the girl, and added after a long pause: 'My name is Lakshmi. Oh, my name is Lakshmi,' she repeated, as if this would explain unsayable things.

'Two—it means sixty-four ounces,' he said, to prove he had understood.

'What's that?' she asked, playful, hoping he would come and caress her.

'It's just the worth of man plus man—at the ration shop.'

'Why do you work there?' she asked, sitting up. Her breasts drooped a little but were very rapt and succouring, beautiful. Govindan Nair had once wanted to paint.

'Why don't you work in one? We all live on rations,' he said, smiling. 'What is your salary?' he asked.

'Six rupees a day plus tips. Good men are good. Sometimes they even give me a necklace. Look at this one. A Seth from the north gave it to me. (He was a grain merchant.) I did not understand his language. He did not speak mine. But he came back after he had gone, and gave it to me and said: Be happy.'

'Are you happy?' asked Govindan Nair.

The girl threw a bit of her sari over her body.

'Are you?' she asked.

'Can't you see I am happy?'

'Where does it come from?'

'Where does water come from?'

'From the tap?'

'And the water in the tap?'

'From the lake?'

'And the water in the lake?'

'From the sky.'

'And the water in the sky?'

'From the ocean?'

'And the water in the ocean?'

'From the rivers.'

'And the river waters?'

'They make the lakes.'

'And the tap water?'

'Is river water.'

'And so?'

'Water comes from water,' she said.

'I am a kitten,' he said.

She seemed frightened. She covered her pubic parts with her sari.

'What?' she asked.

'I let the mother cat carry me.'

'And so?'

'And the river flows.'

'And then?'

'The lakes give water to taps.'

'Then?'

'Man is happy—because he knows he lives in a house three storeys high. When his woman is going to have a child, he will build a house two storeys high. He will marry her and build his child a house. The child, the child, he cries as if in tragic tenderness, the child will have a house to grow in. Oh, children need houses. And women need husbands.'

'I had a husband,' she said. 'Yes,' she insisted.

'What happened to him?'

'He died in the wars.'

'Who killed him?'

'The British.'

'Why?'

'Because he would not shoot at the Germans.'

'And how did you come here?' he asked.

'And how did you come here?' she replied.

'I came because I work in a ration office. I distribute physical happiness to him that wants.'

'And not to her that wants?'

'I have a she—and she wants it, and I pour it into her. To speak the truth, nobody can give. Only the mother cat can give.'

'Give me!' she cried.

'Come tomorrow to Ration Office No. 66. I will give you a card, a family card. Between ten and five we are always there.'

She sank back on the bed. Govindan Nair observed that she had flowers in her hair. She was gazing at the ceiling. Just a tear or two was dropping, marking her face with collyrium. She looked lovely with her well-knit limbs, her sorrow which heaved her breasts—there was such ovular pain where the centre of her body lay. He put his hand there and said, 'Forgive.'

His touch seemed magical. She flung up and put her arms around him, her breasts against his face. He bowed low, made a namaskar, and stood up. How can man make a woman suffer? How can anyone touch a body so smooth, a face so gentle, so helpless, the Seth's necklace speaking a strange tongue against her imbibing navel? Her hair was so perfect.

'The British did it?' he said.

'Yes. Man did it,' she said.

'May I go? he asked.

'Yes,' she said, like a wife to a husband. Tenderly she rose, covered herself, and stood up like a daughter before a father. He turned as if to hide his emotions. Of course pen and paper were there. Everything was typed and ready. He signed the paper. Ration Shop Licence No. 9181 in the District of Ummathur. In the village of Udasekarapuram. Name of the holder: Prabhakar Pillai. Address: Main Street, Murtarakara. Valid up to August 11, 1944. Signed: B. Govindan Nair. The signature was clear and round as the eyes of a child. Lakshmi was dressed by now. She looked so clean, so like a Brahmin lady near the temple streets.

'Your husband will come back,' he said.

'They shot him,' she said.

'No, they did not. I have the ration cards of all the soldiers. I have his name, I am sure, in the office. Our working hours are between ten and five.'

'Bless me, as if I were your daughter,' she said.

'My sister,' he said.

And when she lifted up her face, her whole being was lucent. She was going to find her husband. Life is like that. You get what you want. But do you know what you want? 'Do you really know? Mister, that is the problem,' said Govindan Nair that evening to me. 'You do not want to build this house. I really want to. Shantha will have a child. She is your wife. A wife must have a house. You have a son. I prophesy,' he said, and jumped across the wall as if carried away like a kitten.

I want to take you to London, will you come? I want to take you to Paris, Delhi, New York,

will you come? Will you truly come? Don't
you hear the koel sing on the coconut tree,
don't you hear the anguish that wants to eat
your heart, cut it and pickle it, and savour
it, and say: Look what a good heart I have. I
am a woman. And I have such a good heart.
What will you give me in return, my lord?
I should give you, woman, a house three-
storeys high. Lord, may that rise. And do
not forget the windows that go running
along the wall towards the sea. I must have
eleven windows on the sea. A window on
the sea is a window on God. Buy me a plot
and build me a house eight directions wide,
and that will have a tamarind tree in the
backyard for the baby's hammock, a row of
dahlias (like Europeans have) in a bed to
the right, and a mango tree that will stretch
and burden itself with such riches that,
when the koel sings, we know its song will
make the fruit ripen. For the woman with
a womb that has grown round, what one
needs is ripe, rich *rasapuri* mangoes. Cut
them, peel the skins off and, Mother, give
them to me on a silver plate. And one cup
of milk immediately after.

71

Oh, Shantha, how beautiful you look in your pregnancy. You look like Panchali herself.

I am no Panchali or Damayanthi, Mother. I am just a woman. Lord, may I just be woman. Let me bear womanhood. He has given me his manhood that my womanhood be. If I were a queen I would build a wall of wattle round the garden and I would then hear the sea. The sea knows me.

White is the foam that goes gathering along the sea, white as the skin of snake, with ripples and soughs, and the last song of despair. The sea lurches and tears from inside. O Sea, where will you take me? Will you take me to the nether world of the Nagas, and tie me a chignon wound into a big bun? I shall wear a large *kumkum* and my ear lobes will touch my shoulders. I want to hold my child so round he would kick ten distances long. I want to love. I want to kiss my child. Lord bear me and build me a house.

Like a pirate on the high seas (at the time of the Dutch, so to say) is Govindan Nair. He can command a crew of ten Mophlas and in any language you like. He could put a bark on to the sea and say: Sea, take it, and the sea would heave and bear you to where the isles are. Truth goes over the sea, for the isles are to be blessed. The seagulls know that truth is a breath of Antarctica. Did you know, for example, that if you stand at the southern tip of Travancore and look down against your nose, straight down lies Antarctica, rich in its fissures of fishes? The fishes of Antarctica are made of gold. Gold is dug there. They discovered a tablet there some years ago which showed they probably wrote in the Dravidic tongue. Antarctica is our home. They used to grow pineapples there. You can find congealed seeds of the lotus in Antarctica. The bones of its people are all long and thin, un-Aryan—their heroes lie beside coconut shields made on tropical seas. I know whence they came. They came from Malabar. Malabar is Truth. Antarctica is only a name for Malabar. So we'll go in catamarans and down the seas to where the isles lie. Let us go and quarry there. You'll see stone there like ice frozen for a million years. It has the colour of human eyes. What a fine thing to build a house of eyes—of kittens' eyes! Lord, the isle is far and I am a man. But, look, look, at the silver bark that stands. Truth goes on a ride. We'll ride with Truth. Ancient temples lie there. Nobody worships there. The seas meet in Antarctica. Lord, help me build a house.

That's what Govindan Nair said coming to see me the next morning. 'Mister, I had such wonderful dreams. I wanted to build you a house in ice and give you a garden. I want to give you a large tree at the back for the child's hammock. And in front a mango for the pickles. Then you will hear a lot of birds. We'll get a pair of peacocks too, and your child will dance. How do you like that?'

Govindan Nair looked indeed as if he had ploughed the seas.

At about nine o'clock in the morning, while we were sitting and playfully gossipping, what should happen but somebody knocked at the door. It was my fat landlord, a towel tied around his head (for he had a bad cold—it had rained a little during the night). He was smoking a cheroot. Morning and evening it never left him. His name was Murugan Mudali and as his name said, he tapped palm trees for toddy—huge lorries and bullock carts carried the white frothing, invigorating drink, and people sang praises of themselves singing songs, and they sang him out money with which he built these houses. He was not a bad man—he was a good man. He thought of the bathroom and the kitchen with such care, every housewife blessed him for it. He even ran a hotel—called the Madhura Town Hotel—and the inmates there spoke so well of the tap that ran with hot and cold water (unknown in Trivandrum, except at the Mascot Hotel, and that is run by the government). Since the war started, he had paid as much as thirty-seven rupees a yard for the Hume water pipes, and that is black-market price. He wanted to be just. He made his seventeen per cent profit—that is what his father and his father's father had fixed in the good old times as decent income on any investment—and the rest he gave to you: 'I spent fourteen thousand rupees on building Kamla Bhavan' (which you remember is the name of the house I live in) 'and, sir, take it for eighteen and three. It satisfied you and it satisfied me.'

'Here are seven,' said Govindan Nair as though he were producing the money.

Usha, who had stayed on with me, was still fast asleep in my room. On hearing the sound of such large sums of money she woke, and came scampering to find out what was going on outside her dream. She knew her father lived in many, many worlds. So Usha said: 'Father, who is this?'

'Your grandfather,' answered Govindan Nair, as if led by intuition. The Mudali was silent, and then with a sigh he wiped the lone tear at the corner of his eye. Why should one not be a grandfather? Is it so difficult a thing? Do not toddy pots get full in the morning, once you tie them to the tree at night? Why should not my daughter bear a child? A child, sir, a grandchild is what man must see to prove he dies well. The question, however, is, Can one die? Must one die?

'This house will be yours, Usha,' said Govindan Nair, and for some reason Usha started shrieking and said: 'Mother take me away. Mother, I want to go home.'

'What is your name, child?' asked the Mudali.

'Her name, sir, is Usha Devi—Usha Devi Pai,' said Govindan Nair.

And taking Usha on his lap, he added: 'And she will be my daughter-in-law. Shridhar is seven years and eight months old. Usha is six years and two months old. That makes a nice match,' said Govindan Nair, stroking her hair. 'I've even thought of their horoscopes. She is Sagittarius and he's Pisces, with Jupiter in the eleventh house. She will make him live long. I want a son that lives long.'

'Are you an astrologer too, Mr Nair?' asked Mudali. 'If stars govern me, then I must know the stars. If the Travancore Police Manual governs all police officers (and the public), then we must know it too. Travancore is a paradise that follows police rules. If the ration department were under the police, there would be no corruption. We'll build a house yet, sir. Then what is your final price?'

'My price is always final.'

'Oho, is that so?' Govindan Nair spoke as if to himself. 'If Usha becomes my granddaughter I will reduce it by five or six hundred rupees.'

'If she lives in your house, she's your granddaughter. So make it seventeen thousand.'

The Mudali somehow consented. Once he gave his word he never changed. So it shall be seventeen thousand. Meanwhile Tangamma was handing down coffee from the wall. It was hot, steaming hot. The Mudali preferred a smoke. When the last cup came, Usha stood under the *bilva* tree and Tangamma had to bend low to give it to the child. Shridhar still had the same fevers.

'When Advocate Krishnan Nair comes, send him here.' 'He's already at the house, reading his newspaper,' said Tangamma.

'Hey!' shouted Govindan Nair across the wall. 'Hey, Advocate, Advocate General, future Chief Justice, please come, sir. We are ready.'

The advocate, impeccably dressed, came, down the wall as if he were coming to perform a marriage. He needed only the copper vessel and the sacred-bark bundle. Why, he even had the bundle. Didn't you see it? Tangamma brought another cup of coffee. She bent down and gave it to Usha. Usha brought it and gave it to the Mudali. The cheroot smoked itself away. We lived in a sort of jabbering silence.

Who was talking to whom? Who talked, in fact? Nobody talked, and we all understood.

By now the cheroot was finished. The coffee, too, was finished. Govindan Nair produced a table, and the advocate took out and placed before us the three-hundred-rupee stamped document. He had written down on a piece of yellow notepaper all about the thirty cents of land in Puttenchentai belonging to Murugan Mudali, and situated in Plot No. 705, Survey number 4176, Municipal number 663. My name was mentioned as at marriage or funeral—father's name, grandfather's name. Usha Devi Pai was the chief character of the story, as it were. The house was bought for her and for seventeen thousand rupees. Including the yield of the coconut trees, etc., etc.

Govindan Nair jumped across the wall and went to the National Typewriting Institute near the Post Office. Meanwhile the

Mudali told me of his wife's grandmother in Madurai who was a great lady and a beauty. They said she could stop a flood with a mantra, such were her looks. She spoke to the Goddess as if she had known her always. She spoke in classical Tamil. In some past life, so astrologers said, she was born a princess and was married off to the Chiefs of Madurai. She walked in the palace as if she knew all of it. From that came their love of houses. The grandmother and her spouse built and built everywhere in Madras, in Mysore, even in Ootacamund. The Mudali and his wife had no grandchildren, although their daughter had done every pilgrimage. She was thirty-seven and no children came. They never made a false statement; they always took seventeen per cent interest. Even so, no child came, and no dream came to make the child come. Sadhus had blessed, and some had even given coconuts with mantras. Nothing happened even after these many holy acts. Well, sir, that is as the Lord Subramanya wishes.

The National Typewriting Institute has a very good reputation for job work. How clear the document was. It made your heart shine gold, such was the excellence of the typing. I put my signature: Ramakrishna Pai. S. Ramakrishna Pai. Then Govindan Nair signed as witness. Usha drew an Om, and Govindan Nair certified her signature. Murugan Mudali carefully shaped his signature, and somehow wept. He just did not know. Tangamma handed over to Usha betel leaves and coconut, and even tobacco to chew. She ran back as Shridhar was in some sort of delirium. The doctor had promised to come at three. Govindan Nair went home and ran back quickly. I entered my room and brought out his seven thousand rupees. Usha handed the money to Murugan Mudali. Within ten months the rest of the money would be paid, in two instalments. The house became mine—I mean Usha's. Murugan Mudali (he was about fifty-five) began to smile, and seemed almost happy now. He took Usha on his lap. Then he lifted her up to his arm. 'What a sweet child,' he said, and stood up. Govindan Nair said: 'She is the true owner.'

'Permit me, sir,' said Murugan Mudali, 'permit me to take the child home. I want my wife and daughter to see her. May I keep her till the afternoon?'

'Of course.'

'But Shridhar is ill. I want to see him,' said Usha. The children had build little stone stands from which they spoke to each other across the wall.

'Shridhar will be well. The doctor is coming,' Govindan Nair assured her.

The Mudali took the child in his arms and, smiling to himself, closed the garden door. Usha was going to see Grandmother. Was she beautiful? Will she give me glass bangles? Will she take me to the temple? 'Grandfather,' she said, 'will you take me to the temple just once?'

'Why, we'll go now. We'll go home and take Grandmother. We'll go to the temple,' he said.

How beautiful the god was you will never never know. The god lay on his seven-headed serpent. His one wife at the feet and another rising from his lotus navel—blue he lay and in deep sleep. Grandfather wept profusely. One weeps in temples. Grandfather and Grandmother went then to Chalai Bazaar and bought Usha two ankle bands of silver. She looked so lovely she wanted to go back to the temple.

There's only one depth and one extensivity and that's (in) oneself. It's like a kitten on a garden wall. It's like the clock of the Secretariat seen through a mist of clouds—time moves on according to a moon (and the sun) but the offices go on working, people scribbling, smoking, typing, belching, scratching, farting big, fibbing, exuding asafoetida perspiration or the acrid smell of buttermilk—there will be peons to whom a rupee warrants well, but two warrant more, and up the staircase you go, one, two, and three, and each step is worth a rupee, on to the first floor. On the second floor the prices are higher. You pay ten rupees a step. And on the third, it's like offerings to the Maharaja, you pay according to ceremony. And above it all sits time like a nether world recorder asking no questions. It revolves on itself and when the hour comes it strikes. And off it goes—something. What is it that is gone?

What is time? What is death? In fact you could ask what is life. You issue a ration card. Your house number, numbers of the family, are all indicated: you are class A, B, C or D. You buy what you want and when you want, but only what is available. Governments are notoriously mismanaged. A railway car might have gone off to Coimbatore containing rice for Cannanore or Conjeevaram. What matters is that the station begins with a C. Cannanore, Conjeevaram, Coimbatore. It would almost make a nice mantra. Life is only such a mantra—you go on saying life life, or in Sanskrit *jeeva jeeva* (and in Sanskrit it sounds more real), so you go on living. *Jeeva* is life. So I live. There is a clock tower. Then there is the ration shop. Ration Office No. 66 is just above it. The Revenue Board is under the clock tower, and that is where I work. Down the road that goes to the hospital is Ration Office No. 66. That is where Govindan Nair works. His face is full now. I have a house. I have laid the foundation for myself—and through time. The Secretariat clock will go on chiming forever, and as long as it chimes, it will go on telling you the time forever; can you imagine a state without a government? You must have permanence. So permanence is the Secretariat with the clock tower. I hear the clock chime at night from my house. Thus I live a bit of eternity. My house has a garden wall. There is, as you know, a *bilva* tree by the wall. A hunter once broke twigs off the *bilva*, you will remember, and down the leaves fell on the oval emergence of the alabaster. Shiva was pleased with this unknowing worship. I look towards the garden wall. Lord, I am not even a hunter that in his nervousness lets down *bilva* leaves. Lord, what hope is there for me?

Govindan Nair always appears at such a moment. These are the sort of thoughts that run through me in the morning. I usually wash my face and feet. Then I go to the Home Friends for my coffee and *upma*. By the time I return the *Malayalarajyam* is on my veranda. I read it from beginning to end, about Hitler and the wars, Churchill and the speeches, and then I begin to scratch the curve of my feet. I have a house now, my own. Usha is lying inside. She will wake soon and say, 'Father.' What a mysterious word it is.

'Father,' she says. As if I were able to be the cause of anything. For father simply means cause of her. And the cause of cause, what is it? Is it not she? Could there be a father without a daughter? What would Usha be without me? What would this house be if I did not own it? It is not possible not to own it and yet it would somehow be mine? Air I own not, yet I breathe. I breathe myself. Do I own I?

Such are the terrible thoughts that oppress me. Govindan Nair is my guide. He lives across the wall, and the *bilva* spreads like a holy umbrella above him. It gives him spiritual status.

So Govindan Nair comes and says: 'Mister, I am in grave trouble.'

'What?' I ask.

'My son is seriously ill.'

'What illness? For days he's had no fever.'

'Shantha is there. She will tell you.'

'But what is it?'

'It's called fever. But it might any day be called pneumonia.'

'How did it come?'

'Just as its name came. From somewhere.

He was convalescent. He played in the rain planting roses. He got wet. Then he came here and stood talking to Usha across the wall. So you could say Usha gave it to him.'

'What?'

'Since you want a cause, anything is the cause. The more innocent a thing, the more mysterious its cause. You wear a Gandhi cap—a two-anna piece of one-foot cloth that any man can put on his pate, and not even what his irreverent bladder empties could be held in the cap's depth, such its size—yet you could get arrested for anti-British activity. Innocence is the most dangerous thing in the world. So Usha is the cause of Shridhar's illness.'

'Don't make fun of me. Tell me seriously.'

'I speak seriously, sir. All I say is serious. If not, would I blow my precious foul breath to the world?' He looked almost angry. 'Do you think I joke when I say Usha is the cause of my son's illness? She is six years old. He is seven years old. They stood under the *bilva* tree and said many serious things. Did you know what they said to one another? She touched his cheek and said: 'You are like my brother.'

And he said: 'Father says you are my wife.'
And she became so shy, she ran away. So
off he ran, Shridhar, to Shantha, and said:
'Mother Shantha, make Usha my wife.' He
stood silent and, with closed eyes and folded
hands, prayed. She said: 'Why not when you
grow up? When the koel is big it makes a
nest. When the koel is big and another koel
comes, they make a bed to which eggs are
born. When you can build a nest, you will
marry Usha.' 'But Usha has a house now,'
he said. 'Can I not be married now that
she has a house? And we will grow eggs. '
Usha got fever that night. She thought she
was growing eggs. Next morning she went
to the latrine. She was so afraid she threw
off her eggs. She is all right now. Shridhar
got the new disease. He does not know how
to throw it off. I must buy him a house
too, perhaps,' said Govindan Nair, and was
silent for a while. 'It's a good idea if I tell
Shridhar: Shridhar, I will buy you a house
also, and this might get him to feel better.
When you have a house in prospect, your
heart pumps good blood. Yes, that's the
trick. Thank you for the thought,' he said,

and, jumping across the wall, he was gone. Was I responsible for his thought? Was I responsible for Usha's birth? Was I? Was Usha responsible for Shridhar's illness? So I am the sole responsible person. Lord, where shall I go now? For I am cause.

Usha woke up in a delirium. She has been saying she wants to go to the sea. She sees big ships sail. She sees faces of men that frighten her. 'I don't want to go, Mother, I don't want to go with the Dutch!' she shrieks. Her mother always said to the children: 'If you cry, I'll give you away to the Dutch,' and that's why the child cried so. It must be strange to go in Dutch ships across the seas.

'The fever ran high,' said Shantha to me in the evening. Because of Shridhar's fever, Shantha started sleeping in this house. You see, Usha bought this house (though the two instalments have yet to be paid—but the Mudali has given his heart away to Usha), so the house is Usha's and Shantha will come, for Usha is a grown-up child, and she loves her mother, who is Shantha, for Shantha is kind, and will not talk of the Dutch. She who does not talk of the Dutch is Mother, so

Mother is Shantha. And Shantha is round and will give Usha a brother. Will he be like Shridhar? Shantha says Shridhar raves all night. Ice bottles are placed on his head. Dr N.O. Pillai is an able doctor, he never does anything wrong. People live who live. Those that are taken away go away. Look at it in the hospital. Can you prevent what has to go? Tangamma has a difficult time. When her husband is unhappy he is angry. When he weeps he is happy. That, sir, is the law of kitten, he says in philosophic explanation. He has an explanation, as I told you, for everything. Usha is the cause of Shridhar's fever, is as simple for him as the buffalo is the mother of the grey-white calf, suckling at her udder. How mysterious life is. Does one know anything?

The doctor knows. The temperature is measured with a glass instrument that speaks. Modhu, the elder son of Govindan Nair, who is always on the football field or at some decisive mischief (for he wants to be a soldier like Major General Auchinleck), cleans the thermometer and the temperature has gone up to 105 degrees. Hope is a bubble that is born in the heart. It bursts when it will. That depends on the outer air, I think. Or it is like a bad scale? It always shows you a measure according to the ration card. The rice you eat at home belongs to another measure. Hence there is famine. Hence people die.

Famine is the cause of death. Wars are the cause of murder. Imperialism is the cause of slavery. Sri Krishna is the cause of Mahatma Gandhi. Lord, how can man be free from birth and death? Why should death come to our door?

But Shantha is all apprehensive. What if death came not to the next door but to mine—to Usha, I mean? She prayed therefore there should be no death.

But I ask of you, Will death come and say: May I come, sir, dear sir? What is death to a kitten that walks on the wall? Have you ever seen a kitten fall? You could fall. I could fall. But the kittens walk on the wall. They are so deft. They are so young. They are so white. The mother cat watches them. And when they are about to fall, there she is, her head in the air, and she picks you up by the scruff of your neck. You never know where she is. (Who has ever seen her? Nobody has.) To know where she is, you have to be the mother's mother. And how could that ever be? Mother, I worship you.

The bamboos were already in the courtyard. Death had come. It spoiled the nice courtyard, with flowerbeds of roses.

I never went across the wall. How could I? I could hear Tangamma weep, then Govindan Nair said something. Dr N.O. Pillai is such an able man. He walked out of the house efficiently. It was a bad case, he said. His Gladstone bag was so knowledgeable. It contained mysterious instruments that spoke. Death is such speech? Tangamma did everything as if she were sleeping. She did not weep any more. Modhu wept and wept. He had lost his only brother.

Where is Shridhar gone? Where is my friend gone? Usha walked with me, erect and tearless, holding my hand, to the cremation ground. It was decided to burn him though he was only seven. Usha thought it a grand thing to be burned. It made you see your heart. 'Father, where has Shridhar gone?' 'Daughter, he has gone to build a house.'

'Father, where shall we go?' 'Daughter, where there is a house.' 'Father, what is death?' 'Daughter, it's like the clock tower of the Secretariat. It chimes time.' 'Father, what is life?' 'Daughter, it is where no flame can burn.' 'Father, where is that?' 'Daughter, I do not know. Ask Govindan Nair.' 'Father, what is marriage?' 'Daughter, it is when I give you to God.' 'Father, when will you give me to God?' 'Daughter, tomorrow.'

Somehow after Shridhar died Usha stayed on with me. There must always be a kitten on the wall.

Shantha, more and more, came to live with me. The child would soon come. It will be a son. It will be a brother. Usha was going to have a brother. She told her school—now she went to the convent school—that she was going to have a brother. They said: Where is your mother, then? She said: Here. Where do you come from, then? Did you not say you came from Alwaye? She said: Yes. That was my mother's house. This is my house. My brother will be born in my house. And the schoolgirls thought: What a wonder! Can one have a little brother so easily? Usha's brother will be very beautiful.

The Belgian sisters did not speak of brother's mother. So she wondered why God made some people with speech and others who, talking, had no speech. Only some have brother, and that is the truth, she said to herself, as she entered her arithmetic class.

About three or four weeks later, at the end of September it was—no, in fact at the end of August, for the rains have not ended yet, and the Dussera[12] not yet there—one morning Govindan Nair was arrested at his house. He was arrested on a charge of bribery—a yellowed and much greased document was produced to prove that from some old lady in Vulzehavannoor, three miles from Kurtarakara, he had taken a sum of rupees one hundred and nine. She had a son who ran a ration shop. It could not be more explicit, according to Police Inspector Rama

---

12. Dussera is perhaps the most important festival of India. It takes place after the rains and lasts for ten days, during which worship is made to the elephant, horse, armour, books and the *pipal* tree.

Iyer. He had suddenly grown rich, the son of this old lady. How did this happen? A den of corruption (according to police reports) was discovered. The yellowed document was made out in the name of Meenakshiamma, of Pattadkovil, Vulzehavanoor. She was an elderly lady of fifty-seven. She admitted having given one hundred and nine rupees to Govindan Nair. But that was for the sale of a calf, a heifer, she said. Govindan Nair's family home lay some four miles away, in Valauthoor. She knew Govindan Nair's servant. He was taking a calf to the river. The old lady was going to have a granddaughter. It was going to come in two or three days. 'We must have a heifer when the child is a few months old. The present cow will dry up before long.' So the heifer was bought.

People hereabouts have a superstition. Govindan Nair's family is called the Valauthoor family (they fought in some wars and had some vague privileges), and they are supposed to have one virtue: they never touch anything that does not turn gold. Yet they die all of them in miserable circumstances. Some in distant parts and of vague fevers, others of murder or of debauchery, but one and all end badly. Only after the seventh generation will the lineage be pure again. It is a curse of one of the elders who had been allowed to die in starvation, while the others were gay with women. This generation will be the last, says the tradition. The rotten chapter will be wiped off the pages of history. Man will turn innocent again.

So the arrest did not come as a surprise. The death of Shridhar was in fact like a precursor of this event. You know you will suffer, so suffering comes and tells you. Whether you sold a calf (or was it pneumonia?), you must play fair. If you trick destiny, destiny tricks you. If you say: I am all right; I am almighty; I am Govindan Nair; I can weigh children in scales, make wayward women fall at my feet—Destiny chooses the exact fact for your redemption. Rama Iyer comes and takes you away to police custody. He is the mildest of police inspectors. But if he has a warrant of arrest, will he stop because he hears Shridhar has died some four weeks ago? Was the calf sold before or after? The question with the law is a question of dates. If you did not murder the moment you murdered, you might never have murdered. How strange it all is. One moment before, you did not commit murder. One while after, you have. What happened between the two? The knife came into the picture. Yes, the knife.

For everybody in Ration Shop No. 66 knew this was all fake. First of all, a man who plays with children so—Kunni Krishna Menon's family will bear you witness to this— could not have sold false permits. How could he starve children? If you starved mothers, you starved children. If you starved fathers, you starved mothers from having children. So you could not starve anybody. Starvation comes only through a man that could, like the British Government, say, I am me, may I alone live. Can you live alone? I am an island. I am king, etc., etc.

The real story of the arrest is this: One morning—it was a month or two after this house had been bought—Govindan Nair went to his office. He was a little late, being held by some friends for a smoke. Then he went in, up and in, and he saw everybody so busy, their papers under their noses, he felt ashamed to be late. Fortunately there were very few people in the ration shop below, and this gave him comfort. Though there was no real connection between the ration office and the ration shop, yet somehow they worked together, like a husband and wife whose stars are different, but from marriage and progeny they go through to the final bamboo processionals and the funeral anniversaries. Thus the two were tied together.

Not finding many persons in the shop below meant the office was running well. There was no overwork. The boss was in a good humour. The fresh ration cards had come in from the printers. Besides, perhaps that rascal Velayudhan Nair's cold is better. Thus he will have started verifying the new ration card numbers. Sometimes the printers deliberately repeated a number and sold the duplicate to hotel servants for ten rupees.

If not, tell me how are the hotels to thrive? Once again, sir, it's a matter of starvation.

So Govindan Nair went in, and what he saw was indeed strange to behold. In a cage of white steel wiring, in fact in a big rat trap, was a large cat, and the cat and the cage were on Govindan Nair's table. His table was totally cleaned up.

In the next room his boss was sneezing away as usual with his handkerchief in his hand—he had put too much snuff into his nose. It comes from living very near the temple, and every Brahmin gives you a bit of snuff: 'I wash the divine vehicles for the Dussera festivals, and here is some snuff for you.' 'I go to pour curry powder for the sacred viands, here's a "pinch", Bhoothalinga Iyer.' 'I am going to wash the second dawn service vessels, and here's "a sniff", Mr Ration Superintendent.'

And so on, up to the bus stop and there is always Vishwanath Iyer, who gives you some when you get on. All the office-going people get in together and snuff together, and by the time the bus has crossed the railway overbridge and passed the office, you have had three pinches. You have to wipe the front of your coat to remove every trace of this dark trituration. It looks disreputable going to the office with a garland of dark powder. Then you go in, and going in you see the cat, you see the cage. Once in your own office, you hear the meow-meow. You say: 'John, what is it?' John the third clerk laughs and hides his face in the palm of his hand. 'Abraham, Abraham!' shouts Bhoothalinga Iyer. Abraham comes in. He too has snuff on his nose. His beard is ever like Jesus Christ's. And he says: 'John has played a trick on Govindan Nair.' 'What trick? A ration office and such tricks. Where are the rats?' 'There are no rats, sir. It's a cat.' ' A cat, when there is no rat? But I thought I saw a rat trap.' 'Yes, sir, but the hook has been removed, and there's a cat.' For Bhoothalinga Iyer rats existed and not cats. Ration shops have rats. That is true. And you must have rat traps. But this meow-meow business—Bhoothalinga Iyer was sure Govindan Nair, that clever rascal (all Nairs have enough Brahmin blood to be clever, Bhoothalinga Iyer used to say, but not enough to understand the truth; truth is the privilege of the Brahmin)—yes, yes, cleverness gone elsewhere always produces these disasters. You have, for example, a cat on your table and in a rat cage.

'John!' he called.

The clerk called, John came in. John had

some money in the Imperial Bank, so he thought himself infallible, he said: 'Yes, sir, what is the matter?'

'What is this nonsense about the cat?'

By now Shivaraman, Syed Sahib and Muthukrishna Pillay had joined him at the door.

'Yes, what is it?'

'Govindan Nair always talks of a mother cat. It carries the kitten by the scruff of its neck. That is why he is so carefree. He says, "Learn the way of the kitten. Then you're saved. Allow the mother cat, sir, to carry you,"' said John, and suppressed his resentful laughter.

Bhoothalinga Iyer was a Brahmin. For him a cat, a *marjaram*, was a pariah animal. It was sly, unclean, unfaithful. It was evil to see a cat first thing in the morning. It was evil if the wretched creature crossed from right to left as you went to office. You had to go back home and visit the sanctuary, and beg the gods to bless you. Then you could catch the bus. Also, cats' hair, if it fell into your milk, was worse than gall. It made you vomit blood. So altogether the cat was not a creature to be thought about. A rat, yes, it was the vehicle of Lord Ganesha himself. In every temple you could see a Ganesha and under every Ganesha there was his vehicle, the rat, like Lord Subramanya had the peacock, or Shiva the bull. But the cat, which god ever rode a cat? Nobody did—so it was improper, unholy, beyond thought. What is beyond thought cannot be thought about—it is evil to the temple street. Evil has a name, a text and a commentary. Can you speak without text? You could therefore never say you can prove the cat is holy. Nobody, no god, rode on it. 'Chee-Chee!' sneezed Bhoothalinga Iyer, contemplating the cat.

Poocha is what a cat is called in Malayalam. But Bhoothalinga Iyer always used the Sanskrit word *marjaram*. It carried its own condemnation. It needed no more explanations. It made you talk less. Abraham understood. John did not.

'Take it away. Throw it on the roof or anywhere you like.'

'Sir, it's a goodly Persian cat, sir. I thought I would make a present of it to my colleague. Have you any objection, sir?'

'What objection can I have that you give a present to your colleague? Notorious are the Nairs for the mess they live in. Maybe the cat will clear the rats. Do you know his wife?'

'How would I know her, sir?'

'Your wife might know his wife.'

'Sometimes we meet at the cinema. She is a grand lady and from the Theyoorkovil family. They are well spoken of everywhere.'

'Well, so be it,' he said, and took out his snuff bottle.

That meant you could go. The clerks all came back to their places. They laughed into their files. Each one would look at the other, and when the cat said meow-meow, it meant Govindan Nair would be in at any time and what fun we would have. Only Abraham was downcast. This did not forbode good. He wanted the good spread all over the world. He was doing good distributing rice.

Then they heard the big, thumping steps of Govindan Nair. He always came up the steps two at a time as he did three ration cards at a time. It saves energy and it is such fun, he said. So, he was there before they could say anything. They looked composed and silent, very anxious about the distribution of ration cards in the state of Travancore, Northern Division.

Govindan Nair came to the cage and said: '*Poochi-poochi*. You are a nice fellow. Are you a he or a she?' How could he ask such a question? Govindan Nair's hair stood on end. He closed his eyes. He understood. Now, he reverently opened the cage and, taking his coat off, started stroking the cat. She allowed him to do it, for he had such respect. 'What a nice gift to make,' he said. Unable to control himself, John burst out laughing, holding his belly. 'Meow-meow,' cried the cat, and jumped on the Ummathur District desk. 'Ah, *Poochi-poochi*,' said Govindan Nair, full of tenderness. 'Do not go so far north, my lady. I want to build you a house. Where do you come from?' he said, stroking her again. She jumped on top of the stationery almirah. 'Ugh, ugh, ugh! ' laughed Guptan Nair, the extra clerk, trying to hold his laughter in his pocket. The cat now jumped straight on to Abraham's table. The file threads were red and tassels made them look like toys. The cat started playing. It was obviously a civilized cat. One does not see cats like this everywhere. It must have come from a house with many children. 'Chee-chee!' sneezed Bhoothalinga Iyer. The cat jumped to the ceiling and fell into the outstretched arms of Govindan Nair. John was holding his belly and laughing. His joke had worked. 'There's a letter from the Ration Office, B. Division, Kolayathur. He wants to know the number of sacks of rice sent by the goods train. Was it on this expedition the railway line was waylaid? And the seventeen sacks stolen? He is worried about how the movement of rice came to the knowledge of the public,' said John.

Putting the cat back into the cage, Govindan Nair laughed and as if he were spitting out his cigarette stump, he said: 'You.'

'I what?'

'Yes, you what? This is the question,' he said, coming to John's table with perfect equanimity.

'I don't understand,' said John, standing up.

'I am not your boss, sit down,' he said,

putting his hand on his colleague's shoulder. 'You have money in the Imperial Bank.'

'Yes, so I have. My father left me an estate.'

'My father, sir, also existed. Otherwise I would not be here. And he also had a patch of land. I also sold some bit of it lately. It bought a house. But I have no money in the bank.'

'So what? I just don't understand.'

'Abraham understands,' he said, turning aside. Abraham had left his work and come to help anyone in need.

'Nair?' shouted Bhoothalinga Iyer. He was a good man but he wanted obedience from his subordinates.

'Yes Sir,' said Govindan Nair, going towards the boss's office. The cat was saying 'meow-meow'. John went over to Govindan Nair's table and placed the cage on the floor, between the table and the almirah, well hidden away, so to say.

'Nair, who brought this cat here?'

'That is the question I wanted to ask you, sir. I wondered why cats run into such holy places.' Govindan Nair knew the sensibilities of his boss.

'Why do you think this office is holy?'

'Sir, it is holy because we feed the starving. That which feeds the starving is holy. That which feeds the thirsty is sacred. That is why we worship the cow. This shop, this office is a very Kamadhenu.[13] We give what others want.'

'I can't spend my morning arguing mythology with you.'

'Is there anything you want done, sir?'

'Yes. Look into that Ummathur file. The seventeen sacks of rice lost from the goods wagon. The police were here yesterday evening. Please inquire.'

'I'll look into the papers immediately, sir, and let you know.'

Such matters were always entrusted to Govindan Nair. He had studied law up to the first year. He was too lazy to appear for the second year, so he became a clerk. Jobs are going at the Secretariat, war jobs, said a friend. He went in and came out with an order of appointment as it were. So I was

---

13. A legendary cow that gave one everything one wished for.

saying, Govindan Nair knew a bit of law. Also as a student he was a grand speaker, and he was invited by schools for debates. That gave him a wide knowledge of Travancore. And when he married, his father-in-law was a subcollector. This took the father-in-law almost everywhere. This took Tangamma everywhere. So Govindan Nair learned a great deal about Travancore. And then he was a clever man. Hence these files went to him.

The Ummathur-seventeen-sacks case became famous. Even Madras got worried about it. Where had the sacks gone?

The office settled down to peaceful work now. The day was getting hot. The boss started calling for files. Downstairs, the scale made the usual ding-dong noise. Some people spoke in high voices and others at tangents. It was a Saturday morning, so there were not many people. Many of them had gone to the Kalayodhan fair. The rains would stop. The harvest would ripen. And the world yet be fair.

The cat lay upon its belly, its eyes wide and absolutely at rest. It did not say 'meow' even once after that.

Mother cat sits in a cage between the office table and the almirah. In the office there are thirteen clerks. And the boss Bhoothalinga Iyer sneezes from his room. His office is partitioned off and has a swinging door. Every time anyone goes in to answer the boss's calls the cat seems to rise up. There's a painful irritating grating—the hinges have not been oiled. When the boss calls and the hinges creak, the cat sits up on her haunches, then lies down again. When Govindan Nair lifts her cage (for it's a she; after all, one discovered it) mother cat lifts up her head and says 'meow-meow.' Then, bending down, Govindan Nair gives his pen nib to her and she chews it. 'Ah, she chews the origin of numbers,' says Govindan Nair, to whom every mystery seems to open itself. If Lavoisier, as textbooks say, divided oxygen and hydrogen after years of experimentation, our Govindan Nair born in France would only have had to stand and say: 'Water, show thyself to me!' And hydrogen would have stood to one side somewhat big and bellied, and oxygen would have curled herself shy at his knees and suddenly gone shooting like a mermaid into the big sky. And he would not have lost his head in the Revolution. The British, too, chopped off their kings' heads. A king chops off your head, or you chop his, but the police state is different from the state Truth policed. The fact is that when the mother cat carries you across the wall and to anywhere, there is nothing but space. Space is white and large and free. Why don't you go there? Sir, you will say, kneading your snuff, but there is a wall. To which Govindan Nair makes answer: Like Usha, why don't you put stones one over the other, and standing under the *bilva* tree, you can speak to Shridhar. You now say: That is why Shridhar died. Usha spoke over the wall and the cat carried him away. Funny, sir, that a child is carried away by a cat. Anyway, tell me where is Shridhar gone? He has gone to a house three storeys high. 'Is that what you say, mother cat?' asks Govindan Nair. The mother cat says 'meow'. Govindan Nair cannot keep her in the cage any longer. He opens the cage and the cat leaps on to his lap. It is a trained cat. It knows what is right from what is wrong.

Children below were playing hide-and-seek among the rice bags. The ration shop was also their play-ground. While the mothers waited, the children played among the bags. Govindan Nair wanted to go down and play with the children, but there was this Ummathur file and the seventeen sacks lost. Who had stolen the sacks? Was it a gang of poor men or was it merchants' marauders? Stroking the cat, his pen in his mouth, Govindan Nair was contemplating. When he thinks in this manner it means he wants to do something mechanical. He always carried a penknife with him, for sharpening pencils and such other things (including rose twigs). He usually took this out, pulled out the blade and started rubbing it up and down the edge of the table. Just where he worked on his files, he had written, or rather carved, many names—his own, the name of his boss, and Usha's (I was surprised once when I went to visit him to find Usha's name there, but it was there). Sharpening the knife, he started humming to himself.

'Hey nonny, nonny, nonny . . .'

Govindan Nair: What a kind thought,

Abraham. Whoever it is that had the idea. I was just thinking this morning. There are so many rats at home. There are so many rats in the office. You remember the Sidpur file? It might have been the rats. Big ones like bandicoots, they be. And then, at home. There are so many. Even they seem to have famine. A country at war has rations. A rationed country has little food. When there is little grain to eat, the rats become courageous. They will bite off anything. Even the nose of a man. *(He looks around him and speaks to John.)* So, I say, thank you for having had such a kind thought, Mr John. *(Everybody bursts out laughing again. The boss also sneezes.)* Thank you, Mr John, for this wonderful gift. A cat, sir, a cat. Now, now let me make a speech in the manner of Hamlet. To be or not to be. No, no. *(He looks at the cat.)*

A kitten sans cat, kitten being the
diminutive for cat. *Vide* Prescott
of the great grammatical fame.
A kitten sans cat, that is the
question. *(He turns the cage round and round.)*

To live is not difficult,
sir, for flesh is the form of
existence, and man in his journey to
the ultimate knows that
to yield to the flesh is to
grow grain. To yield to the pipe
is to blow flame. Asthma is
the trouble that Polonius reveals
for fool; he hid behind the curtain
asthmatic.

John: And what happened to him?

G.N.: Sir, Lady, by now I pierce (*he makes
as if he pierces something with the right arm*)
the veil, and the asthmatic falls. (*A thud.*)

John: Murder, murder.

G.N.: Rank murder.
Rank murder and dark desolation
for Ophelia.

Syed Sahib: Go, get thee to a nunnery.

John: Why, Abraham, that's the place for
you. Isn't that so?

Syed Sahib: To the nunnery, maid (*looking
at the cat*).

G.N.: To the rank growth I go,
Hey nonny, nonny
To the slipping world I go,

113

Hey nonny, nonny.

I tell you what, sir. In the kingdom of Denmark there's one blessed thing. Whatever they are they are not mad. (*Lets the cat out of the cage. It leaps on a desk, familiar, affectionate, but distant. It licks its front paw.*) The kingdom of Denmark is just like a ration office.

John: How so, Mr Nair? That's a great idea—Shakespearean, I should say.

G.N.: Shakespeare knew every mystery of the ration shop. Here however we haven't to murder a brother to marry his wife. Here we marry whom we like. The ration card marries. You are married even when there is no wife. You are married without looking at horoscopes. The dead are not buried in ration shops. There will be no grave scene. Ophelia will die but she will have no skull left for Hamlet, a future Hamlet, to see. We slip, sir, from sleep to wake from wake to sleep. We marry the wife in dream, and we wake up king of Denmark. We marry Ophelia in dream and wake up having a Polonius to bury. We live in continual mystery. In fact I ask you, John, my

114

friend (sharpening his knife on the table), when one commits murder in a dream, is that murder or not?

John (very clever): That's jurisprudence. I'm only a clerk. Y.P. John is only a clerk.

G.N.: I ask you, what is dream? Are you sure you are not in dream (*laughing*)? An asthmatic cough, with the cry of children under the creak of balance, and the cat, a Persian cat on the table of Ration Office No. 66. Is it dream or is it real?

John: Every bit is real, but the whole is not. So it is not a dream.

G.N.: In the dream the whole is real.

Abraham: The boss is worried about that Ummathur file.

G.N. : Are you sure the wagon did not go to Coimbatore? Or did it go to Cannore? Both have C in them. Even when awake we make such an error. The reason, sir, why I ask you 'are you in dream or in waking state?' is simple. In dream the dead appear.

John: That is so. (*The cat comes and lies before Nair. It seems to be listening carefully to what Nair is saying.*)

115

G.N.: In ration offices, as we all know, the
    dead have numbers. Killing be no murder.
John (addressing himself to Abraham): What
    ho, Horatio.

Now, Govindan Nair walked straight over
to John's table. Perhaps he just wanted to
consult a file.

'John,' he said, while the mother cat
stood behind him.

'Yes, Mister,' said John, very sure of
himself.

'John, this is a cat,' he said, lifting up the
cat and placing it on John's table. The whole
office stopped work. Even Bhoothalinga
seemed involved in this silence.

'What's that?' cried Abraham, and came
over to John's table.

'Oh, I am only talking to him about the
cat.'

'What cat?' said Syed, his hand on
Govindan Nair's shoulders.

'Why, man, cat. There's cat only. All cats
belong to one species—cat. Call it cat or call it
mar jara which is Sanskrit or better still *poochi*

which is Malayalam, it's the same—isn't that so, John?'

'Yes, my lord,' said John, rising up from his seat.

'So, gentlemen, I wanted to know how much zoology our friend knew. What is a Persian cat called in Latin? In fact what is the Latin name for a cat?'

'*Felinus*,' said Abraham, remembering his church instructions.

'Then *felinus persiana* would be a Persian cat,' said Govindan Nair, who knew of course everything.

'Yes,' said Abraham dubiously.

'And man?''

'*Humanus.*'

'And I?' he said.

'*Ego.*'

'Make me a Latin sentence, Abraham. *Ego esse humanus malabario et lux esse felinus persiana*, or some such thing.'

'I don't know that much Latin,' said Abraham.

The curious thing was that the boss did not call. The cat continued to raise her tail and bunch herself to be caressed. Govindan

Nair still held the penknife in the other hand as if it were his pencil. Man must hold something with his hands, otherwise how could he know what he is about? If you carry a penknife like a pencil in your hand you are a clerk. Is there any doubt about it? 'Speaking biologically,' Govindan Nair used to say, 'a hundred generations of clerks will secrete lead from their bowels and clerks' fingers will bear capillaries like those in the new office pencils. You write morning, noon, and night. You could even write in your dreams.'

'What is clerk in Latin?'

'*Clericus* is Latin itself.'

'Ha, ha,' said Govindan Nair. Seeing the whole office around him, and the boss silent—it was a hot morning—he added: 'Define the cat, Mr John.'

'Mr Govindan Nair, a cat is a feline being.'

'What are its characteristics?' Govindan Nair started making a firm and rapid movement with his knife (back and forth), as if he were sharpening the pencil on the beautiful skin of the cat.

'Its characteristics are—its characteristics

are,' mumbled John, and as somebody said, he had cleared his bladder audibly. It poured an acrid smell into the room. Bhoothalinga Iyer had a bad cold, and one could hear him snuff in snuff. There was such silence in the office (but for the burring sound of Govindan Nair, who always burred anyway) that Bhoothalinga Iyer was sure everybody was at work. There was suddenly silence even in the ration shop. And this was the sort of silence which sometimes rises like a temple pillar from earth to heaven; all creation seems still, as if the universe pondered: What next?

'First of all, it's of the same family as the lion,' said Rama Krishna, a young clerk. He had joined them only three months ago, fresh from college.

'Then?' asked Govindan Nair.

'Then,' said Abraham, getting very anxious, 'it goes in and out of one's house as not even a man can.'

'What very intelligent colleagues I have,' remarked Govindan Nair, smiling. 'Then?'

'A cat is the purest animal in the world.'

'Why so? Hey, there, Syed, what does your Muslim theology say about it?'

'In Muslim theology only the chameleon is evil. It betrayed Muhammed. And the hog. But the cat, it is sacred.'

'No, man, I know your theology better. The cat is not sacred in Islam. It is sacred in Egypt. It was called Bastet.'

'And it wore a crown?' said John, a little reassured that all this was a joke.

Govindan Nair quickly made a paper crown; he cut the three sides of a triangle and gave it a point, and placed it on the head of the cat and said: 'Hey, Bastet, you are sacred, don't you understand?

'And, Syed, what is it your people do when what is sacred is treated as what is sacred?'

'We kneel and touch the ground and ask for Allah's blessings.'

'Now, Mr John, you understand. Here is Bastet. You have brought a very god to our poor ration office. You be the priest.'

'Oh, no,' said John. He knew Govindan Nair had something up his sleeve.

'Kneel!' shouted Govindan Nair. 'Kneel, man!' And he brandished his knife, holding the cat firmly with his left hand. 'Or say: No sir, I am a low-born, I am a coward. Kneel!' he shouted. Bhoothalinga Iyer's chair creaked. 'You don't insult a cat like this, stuffing a cat into a rat cage.'

John knelt devoutly.

'There, once again,' shouted Govindan Nair.

John knelt again, crossing himself. Syed had his hands brought together. All the office was one noumenal silence.

'Kiss it,' shouted Govindan Nair again.

John kissed the cat. Bhoothalinga Iyer came and stood behind the crowd. He thought some file was being tampered with.

'Govindan Nair!' he shouted.

'Yes, sir.' And Govindan Nair went towards his boss. The cat jumped down the table and everybody gave way to the cat. By now she's lost her crown. Rubbing against his legs it cried meow, meow and Govindan Nair lifter her up and placed her on his shoulder with his right hand. His knife was still in the left.

'What is this?' asked Bhoothalinga Iyer.

'We've been discussing the Latin formation for Persian cat. Do you know it, sir?'

'In Sanskrit it is called *marjaram*,' he said as if he were saying it with only the tip of his tongue. 'And for Persian cat there's no word in ancient Sanskrit.'

'In Malayalam it is called *poochi-poochi*,' said Govindan Nair, as he went back with the boss to the inner office.

The boss sat down in his chair.

The cat jumped on to Bhoothalinga Iyer's table. It saw another tassel of a file and started playing with it. Bhoothalinga Iyer, seeing all the eyes of the office (for everybody, as it were, came to see what was happening), wanted to shout: Get out! Get away! But his tongue would not say it. How can you say with what is not what is? How can you shape words that cannot come from yourself? What do you do if you find yourself a prisoner? You want to escape. Govindan Nair laid the knife on the table and said to Bhoothalinga Iyer: 'Sir, tell me a story.'

'What story?'

'Any story.'

'I know no story.'

'I'll tell you a story,' said Govindan Nair, and lifted the cat and placed her on his shoulder.

'Once upon a time,' he began, and before he could go on, the cat jumped on to Bhoothalinga Iyer's head. Bhoothalinga Iyer opened his eyes wide and said, 'Shiva, Shiva,' and he was dead. He actually sat in his chair as if he could not be moved.

Govindan Nair rushed back home with the beautiful Persian cat in the cage and let it loose in the house. Then it was he went to Bhoothalinga Iyer's funeral. Bhoothalinga Iyer's wife, Lakshamma, was moved, deeply moved, by all the consoling words Govindan Nair spoke to her. He spoke of death and birth and such things. He too was weeping. His boss had died. Bhoothalinga Iyer had asthma. And asthmatics have weak hearts. And the snuff did not help, did it—said the Brahmins at the door of the temple.

For some strange reason, everybody came to console Govindan Nair at his office as if he had lost something. Kunni Krishna Menon from the next house came and spoke as though Govindan Nair needed condolence. Perhaps he would be promoted to his boss's place—there was such a rumour.

Then he could not run down and play with the children, remarked Abraham. An officer could not do it. 'Then you be boss, Abraham,' said Govindan Nair, hugging him.

With two deaths within forty days Govindan Nair moved about in a bemazed state. He had loved Bhoothalinga Iyer, and true, it was the cat that had jumped on the boss's head. But who had brought in the cat? John, of course. And Bhoothalinga Iyer had no business to be asthmatic. And so the boss died. Usha talked across the wall to Shridhar, and he died. True, you call it pneumonia (Dr N.O. Pillai said so), but Shridhar died. Thus Govindan Nair made Abraham the chief, and had him so nominated. He preferred, did Govindan Nair, to be clerk. People said this and that, and they said now Govindan Nair can go on building houses. A boss cannot do it. Govindan Nair said, 'To be a boss one has to be asthmatic or diabetic,' and everybody laughed. For Abraham could not live without insulin.

Abraham was withal an able officer. He bought himself a new (second-hand) bicycle, a green B.S.A., and when he came to office he looked like a padre going to his flock.

Abraham's strength was that he was a good man. If good men did not run ration offices who should? This was the argument of Govindan Nair. We should not all become British agents. So Bhoothalinga Iyer's widow was given rice as if Bhoothalinga Iyer were still alive. Where after all could the poor man have gone, with the scarf on his head (tied tight like a turban), and his perpetual cold because of snuff, and his love for service regulations, Section No. 345 of the Travancore Civil Service rules, etc.? Yet he did not die a gazetted officer. He might have, had he lived longer.

Ration cards for orphans and such others were not looked into too carefully. You gave a card eventually to those who needed it. The rascals were there for the rest. Someone will always build a temple spire to expiate his sins. Man has a heart white as a rice pod but he makes it dark as a lentil pod, for he thinks the world is a scale, and the master weigher is not Abraham. Lord save us from our sins. Lord, may rice be rice, and lentil be lentil. That is the secret of the world. You want to make the rice lentil. Botanists will tell you, rice is *Oryza sativa* and lentil *Lens esculenta*. How can the *sativa* become *esculenta*? How can two not seek the not-two? Find this secret and you need no gold to seek happiness.

Govindan Nair brought back the cat and gave it to me. Somehow he thought I would look after it well. 'I look after a cat?' I said. 'Ask Saroja and she will tell you,' Govindan Nair said. 'Don't ask Saroja, ask Shantha,' and Shantha said that I love cats. Do I? If anyone tells you, you are a rascal, can you prove that you are not? How do you know? What do you really know? Can a rascal see his rascalry? How could he, poor man? So if Shantha says I love cats she must be right. After all, she is seven months pregnant and she must know it better than I. They say pregnant women are holy. They have second sight. Does Usha think I am what I am? She thinks I am her father. How do I know I am her father? Because she tells me so. Because Saroja said: 'This is your child,' when I went back on leave two months after the child's birth. 'This is your child,' she said. She must know. Who knows, anyway? Knowledge alone knows. So how shall I ever know if I love cats? I must know cats and I must know that I know that I love cats. When cats are there, where am I? When I am there, what becomes of the cats? 'It is not easy, Shantha, to say I love cats.' 'But,' she protests, 'Govindan Nair says you love the cat. That is why he had the wall cut just where the stones stood for Usha to speak to Shridhar. When you can walk to the next garden, you can say "I love the cat." Can you not say I love I?' 'No, Shantha, I love you.' Shantha says: 'Good it is that I am a Hindu woman and you are my lord. If I were not that, but one of those big-bosomed women of the European films, smoking and kissing in public, I would not say yes to you all the time, I would say no.' 'Then what is it you want to say, you my Hindu wife?' 'I say, to say I love you is to say I love myself.' 'Who said so, Shantha?' 'Sage Yagnayavalkya said so.' I now understand. Yes, I love Shantha because she has my child in her. That is the secret. She has myself in her.

127

The cat came in and pawed the rug on the floor. The cat was not pleased with something. 'What is it doing, Shantha?' I asked. She said: 'It is asking for its mate.' 'Where shall we find a mate for her, Shantha?' 'She knows herself where it is to be found. She knows the self. So she is the self.'

Shantha is always mysterious. Just as Saroja was always clear. Shantha always says two things at the same time. No wonder she and Govindan Nair like each other so much. She says: 'How can anything mean one and one thing? Look at the *bilva* tree. It's *bilva* tree all right. But were there no light, would it be a *bilva* tree? So when you say it's a *bilva* tree, that means there is the tree and the light that makes it the tree.' 'If I touch you, Shantha, there is no light in that.' She said: 'I can see you have never been across the wall. For there you could touch me and see yourself touch me.' 'What, what's special about that?' 'The specialness is that it is not special. You think because I bear a child I am special. Very, very special, my lord.' 'Yes, you are.' 'But you know, as I teach in my school, all that is born had a mother. The father is not always so clear. Look at the bees and the flowers.' 'So the mother is necessary for all children. Thus motherhood has nothing special. And what about fatherhood, Shantha?' 'Don't you go on teasing me. Show me the proof of your fatherhood. You have a belly small as a cucumber,' she said and laughed. 'Yes, that is true. Where is the proof of my fatherhood?' She said: 'There is proof.' 'Where is it, Shantha?' 'I am your proof. You are only seen by me. Who could know you as I know you? So the proof of my lord is me. The proof became concrete and became the child. I must know I am. You made me say I am.' 'Who says I am, Shantha?' 'Nobody, and that is your proof. Only I say you. And you say I. That is the proof of proof,' she said, and became very silent.

That's always the difficulty with Shantha. She speaks true. She always speaks in puzzles. And when I ask her why, she says woman is the biggest puzzle. Is that a proof of proof? No.

So, I was saying Govindan Nair brought the cat and left it with me.

Two months later Shantha gave birth to a

129

lovely child. From the moment he was seen, we said, 'Why not call him Krishna?' He was so blue, and her father was called Krishna Pillai. She loved her father, so she loved me. I loved the child, so the child loved her. The father, did he love me? Poor man, he was dead and so long ago. Was he reborn as the child to love me? Who knows? Shantha's mother said our Krishna looked just like his grandfather. After all, you see what your eyes see. That is the root of the problem, said Shantha. So we gave the child no name.

I should be happy with the child, with Usha who had returned to me after spending the Christmas holidays with her mother, and the cat. But I can never be happy. How can you know you are an Indian? You must know India. If I am to be happy I must know happiness. What is happiness?

Govindan Nair's definition is, of course, simple: The mind that is not when the cat carries the kitten, that is happiness. That's not very clear. It is just like saying, my nose is that which I catch by carrying my hand behind my head, and turning round quickly hold a facial projection which could be called my olfactory organ. Strange, such roundabout definitions. Man, do two and two make four or not?

'First tell me what two is, and I shall answer the rest,' he said, and laughed. 'You *is* one. I *is* one. Where is the two?' he asked. I heard the baby cry, so I went to give the feeding bottle to him. And I sang a song and sent the baby to sleep:

Jo, jo, push the cradle, jo,
push the cradle of Sri Rama,
push the cradle of Victorious Rama,
push the cradle of Sita's Lord, Rama,
push the cradle, jo.

I sing of man because he is my neighbour. After all, one's big neighbour is oneself. The neighbour's neighbour is always the Self. I speak of the wall and the cat which make the world I live by. Usha is my daughter, and she has a bad cold and is in bed. Shantha's child is two months old, and still we've given him no name. 'Call him man. Mister,' says Govindan Nair. For him, nothing is

131

particular, a chair means all chairs, a knife means all knives, a clerk means all the clerks that go on bicycles to offices, sneezing and wheezing like Abraham. Even a bicycle for him means only a B.S.A. Shall I call my son man? I have made a secret vow. If Govindan Nair is acquitted (for alas, he was arrested by Rama Iyer, not on a charge of attempted homicide, which would have been legitimate, but on a charge of bribery with the one-hundred-nine-rupees document), I'll call the boy Govinda, Govinda, but from the way Govindan Nair laughs and teases Rama Iyer one knows the case is lost. As I told you, Govindan Nair had passed his first year in law. Besides, he was born as it were for argument. He could never see anything except in definition of its situation. If I said, for example, the *bilva* tree, his mind would not think of Shiva and the hunter, as it would occur to you and to me, but he would think of the manure the tree must have had (rotten banana leaves, of course), and of the man who planted it and was it morning or evening when it was planted. The man who had planted it became so important that I teased him often and said the mother is more important than the son. Yes, he said, that is so. The kitten is held at the scruff of the neck by the cat. Who is more important, sir? How can you argue against that?

In fact I used to send food to Govindan Nair at the Central Jail. He said, 'When you were ill I sent you food (and Shridhar came to you), and now I am ill (for what is jail but a philosophical illness?), you send me food, and Usha.' The face of Usha made Govindan Nair happier than anything on earth. He was convinced Usha was Shantha's child. That was again the way with him. If he saw black and found it brown, he could prove it was brown because he saw only brown. His argument was so simple: 'Is there seeing first, or the object first? If I have drunk a glass of coffee with milk and in actual fact I have not, but believe I have, which is more real, my exhilaration or the coffee that was drunk? Proof is only oneself. Proof simply means I know. So brown is brown. Don't you believe you exist, even though you know you will die? How do you say that, Mister? When you know this rotten fat thing, with pus, blood, excreta, with semen for procreation, and bile for digestion, with the five sheaths and the nine supports (called *dhatus* by our forebears), the blood that oozes to the heart and the urine that is thrown out—this filthy sack of the five elements, what does it become? It stinks, sir, it stinks when it is laid on fire. It not only stinks, but as in the case of Bhoothalinga Iyer, it sits up suddenly in the middle of its end, it sits up, and one would think it was going to shout an order: Hey, there (sneeze, sneeze, two sneezes are good)! Hey there, bring me the Ummathur file and seventeen sacks of rice gone—and yet it's a half-corrupt, half-burned thing purring with many fluids. "Chee-Chee!" This body. And this mind, with its encaged gramophone record, another His Master's Voice, and all it needs is a white dog listening to its music. Yes, that's the mystery, sir. The dog listens to this mechanical music. Hey, ho, you say:

> I see waterpots,
> Going to the Ganges, my love
> I see my maid going to
> The morning of marriage, etc., etc.

And you hear the gramophone. The difference is not only that you have to change the record. You have to change the needle as well. But whether you sing a cinema song or you sing a hymn to Shiva, the box is just the same, only the needle talks to the record. Who made the record? Eventually you made it, for you go to buy it, and he who sells it made it because you will buy it, and he who sings knew there would be a buyer, so you are the cause of the song. Now sing, Man:

> I am empty as a tamarind seed,
> The lord plays the square and
> four with me.

That is right. When you are reminded that you are empty as a tamarind seed, you see it and say it again, you know the tamarind seed is empty. And begin to think of the play. And where play begins, reality begins. Reality is only where you go to prison and say, close the door and open the door. Any door can open and any door can close. What is special about a prison door that you call it prison door? In dream you must have gone to a house from which you could not escape.

The staircase fell off and the upper wall had gone somewhere. On waking up, do you say, I am falling, I am falling? You say, I played in the dream. You go to the office and go up the staircase with the ration shop below (and its huge scale), and you put your coat down and sharpen your pencil and say: Let me look into the Ummathur file. Then suddenly you remember that in the dream Bhoothalinga Iyer was shouting, "Nair, Nair, I missed my train to Coimbatore. What shall I do?" Did he miss his train to Coimbatore? Is that what he wanted to say on getting up and sitting on his pyre? Where has he gone? Where has Bhoothalinga Iyer gone? Lord, do you know?' etc., etc.

There is no argument against a man like Govindan Nair, who will bring a staircase from his dream to prove that Bhoothalinga Iyer has gone to Coimbatore. His further argument is: Prove to me that Bhoothalinga Iyer is not in Coimbatore.

You may say he is talking nonsense. No sir, he is talking sense. You never saw a man talk more sense than Govindan Nair. Even Usha says she can understand him. I cannot. Shantha can, and the cat seems to understand. But I read *The Hindu* too much, that is the trouble with me, and I cannot understand. What can *Malayalarajyam* say, except what its correspondents see? But Govindan Nair talks of only what he sees. That means he does not talk. And this is the secret of his state.

The white-clad judge, Mr Gopala Menon, said in the palace-like court by the railway line which every advocate knows so well— the name-boards of the advocates look like coconuts on a tree, there are so many in the building across: Vishwanatha Iyer, BSc, LLB; Ramanujan Iyengar, MA, ML, Advocate High Court; Mr Syed Mohammed Sahib, Advocate; R. Gangadharan Pillai, High Court Advocate; S. Rajaram Iyer, Advocate; etc., etc.—the judge said: 'I cannot follow your argument, sir. Will you repeat?'

'Mr Bhoothalinga Iyer, of blessed memory,' Govindan Nair started, 'used to visit certain places whose names are not mentioned in respectable places.' ('Ho, ho!' shouted one or two persons in the gallery.) 'If I do not mention the name, it is because many persons whose faces I see before me now, if I may say so, betake themselves there.'

'My Lord, such insinuations are not to be permitted in open court,' shouted a member of the bar.

'The sun shines on the good and on the wicked equally, like justice. Please go and close the sunshine before you say: this should not be discussed in open court.'

Court: 'The Accused is free to do what it likes.'

'I was only saying: Whether you close the door and sit like photographers in the darkroom or you come out, the sun is always open. The Maharaja of Travancore, sir—'

'Say His Highness.'

'Yes, His Highness the Maharaja of Travancore is there, whether his subjects— say some fellow in the hill tribes—knows his name or not.'

'So?'

'So what is real ever is.'

'That is so,' cried the Government Advocate.

'Yes, but we never want to see it. For example, that a worthy man like Bhoothalinga

Iyer (of blessed memory) used to visit places of little respectability.'

'So?'

'So, he met there, one day, a lady of great respectability.'

'Your statements are so contradictory.'

'Your Lordship, could I say Your Lordship without the idea of an Accused? Could I say respectable without the ideas of unrespectable coming into it? Without saying, I am not a woman, what does the word man mean?'

'Yes, let us get back to Bhoothalinga Iyer.'

'Mr Iyer used to visit such a place.'

'And then?'

'One day after visiting such a place, he met me at the door.'

'Yes, go on. Did he?'

'Of course. I went there regularly. My wife will tell you.'

'Oho,' exclaimed Advocate Tirumalachar from the bar table.

'And at the door he said: "Every time I commit a sin, I place a rupee in the treasure pitcher of the sanctuary. I tell my wife this is for me to go to Benares one day. But the treasure pitcher is tightly fixed with sealing wax. There is here in this place a respectable woman. I like her and she likes me. When I went in, as usual, this time, however, a new woman, a Brahmin woman, I think an Iyengar woman, came. She said her husband was dead. I knew I was going to die soon, being old. But I was in a hurry. So I told her: Do not worry, lady. I will go and tell your husband everything. He will understand. She became naked and fell on the bed. Her breasts were so lovely.'''

'This is sheer pornography,' said an elderly advocate with a big nose.

'I am quoting evidence, Sir,' continued Govindan Nair.

'And she played with her necklace that lay coyly on her bosom.'

'And what did he do?' asked a counsel for the Government.

'He did nothing.'

'Ha, ha, ha,' laughed many of the advocates.

'The dignity of the Court demands better behaviour,' said the Government Advocate. He had never had to argue against so strange a man. He got terrifically interested in his opponent.

'He not only did nothing, sir. Mr Bhoothalinga Iyer was a man of generous heart—'

'To propose immorality as a generous thing!' mumbled Advocate Tirumalachar. Tirumalachar, who looked fiftyish and fair, was known for his deep religious sympathies. He was president of the Radha-Soami Sangh, Trivandrum.

'What do advocates defend ?' asked the judge.

'Morality,' said Tirumalachar, rising and adjusting his turban.

'You defend man,' said the Government Advocate. 'But law says we defend the Truth. The law is right.'

'The Government Advocate has said the right thing. Now, Accused, continue.'

'My Lord, I was saying: One day after the whole office was empty and Bhoothalinga Iyer was alone, he said: "Govindan Nair, stay there. I have a job for you." And he produced the Benares pot that he had hidden deeply in the sample rice sack. There was one sack always in the office. Who would look into it? So he produced the Benares pot and said: "Go to Mutthalinga Nayak Street and in the third house right by the temple Mantap there must be a widow called Meenakshiamma. Please hand over this one hundred and nine rupees. That is all there is in it. I told my wife yesterday to go to the cinema with my son-in-law. She went. I stole this and came here. I opened the office. I had the key. Today I have sent her to the zoo with my son-in-law. Then there is Pattamal's music at the Victoria Jubilee Hall. Therefore they will come late, but I must return home quietly. I know you are a man with a big heart, so please do this service for me. She will wait for you."'

'In English you call this a cock-and-bull story,' said Tirumalachar.

'You could, if you so want, call it a hen-and-heifer story,' said Govindan Nair, and laughed.

'Who then was the witness?'

'As one should expect in such a cock-and-bull story, a cat, sir, a cat,' said Govindan Nair seriously.

The Judge rose and dismissed the court.

He called the accused, and said: 'Please speak the truth.'

And Govindan Nair, with tears running down from his big black eyes, answered: 'Your Lordship, I speak only the truth. If the world of man does not conform to truth, should truth suffer for that reason? If only you knew how I pray every night and say: "Mother, keep me at the lotus feet of Truth. The judge can give a judgement. The Government Advocate can accuse. Police Inspector Rama Iyer can muster evidence. But the accused alone knows the truth.'

'How right you are,' said the judge, flabbergasted. He had never thought of this before. 'Tell me then, Mr Govindan Nair, how can a judge know the truth?'

'By being it,' said Govindan Nair as if it were such a simple matter. After all, he had cut a passage in the wall where Shridhar used to talk to Usha. After all, who could say Bhoothalinga Iyer had not gone to Coimbatore? For example, Abraham could not, as he would lose his job (and with it his green B.S.A. bicycle) if the boss returned. Suppose Shantha's child were really Bhoothalinga Iyer reborn? Who could know? The cat could, was Govindan Nair's conviction.

'Tomorrow I'll bring the cat to court,' he said, as if asking the judge's permission. Of course, what wrong could Govindan Nair have done? Could you ever see a man so innocent? Anybody could see he played with children and the scale. And when one side was heavy, he put two kids on the other side to make the balance go up. Then he brought the needle to a standstill, holding it tight. Thus the balance was created among men. When two things depend on each other for their very existence, neither exists. That is the Law of law.

'The cat, sir, will do it,' he said. The judge consented.

Next day I sent Usha with Shantha (the baby was left at home with Tangamma to look after him). The cat was carried in a big cage.

When the court opened its deliberations, the Government Advocate said: 'My Lord, we are facing judgment against judgment. We must be careful. We have, as witness, a cat.'

'Why not? We are in Travancore.'

'I thought so too, Your Lordship. Why should we follow the proceedings of any other court of the world, were it His Majesty's Privy Council in London? If a cat could be proved to prove any evidence we might set a precedent.'

'My Lord,' said Govindan Nair, rising. Crowds had gathered at the courthouse. Such a thing had never happened before. It was not even a political case. (There was no Gandhi in it.) Women were somehow convinced that Govindan Nair was an innocent man. Some of them had seen him in the ration shop. Others had gone to have ration cards issued. Some had noticed him give way to ladies when the bus was overcrowded. Such things are never forgotten by women. They always feed the child in their womb whether the child be there or not. Who knows, some day . . .

'My Lord, I am not sure this copy of my signature is correct. Could I have the original?'

'The original is in the files,' said the court clerk.

'How could it be wrong?'

The cat escaped from Shantha's hand and ran all over the court. Nobody wanted to stop the proceedings or to laugh. Either would be acknowledging that the cat was there. It went right over to the Government Advocate and sat in front of him as if it were going towards itself. The silence was so clear, one could see the movement of the cat's whiskers. One had no doubt the cat was there. And it knew everything. Each movement was preceded by a withdrawal, recognition, and then the jump. The cat jumped straight on to the judge's table. And before the attendants could brush it away, it leaped down and fell over one of those huge clay office inkpots kept under tables, and, turning through the back door, went into the record room. The court clerk was looking at the file. The cat did nothing. It stood there. The attendants came and stood watching the cat. Then the cat lay down on the floor and started licking its fur. Govindan Nair was burring something in the court. The attendants, seeing the cat doing nothing, went back to the court.

The cat suddenly jumped on to the shoulder of the clerk and started licking his neck. He felt such sweetness in this, he opened file after file. The cat now jumped over to the table and sat. Usha came from the back, led by an attendant, and took the cat in her arms. The clerk had indeed found the paper.

'May I see it, Your Lordship?' asked Govindan Nair.

'Yes, here it is,' said the judge, but at the last moment he held it back. For just as he was handing the paper over, the light from the ceiling—a sunbeam, in fact—pierced through the paper, or maybe it was just electric light. Underneath the signature was another signature. When the judge had read it, he handed it over to the Government Advocate. He read it and said: 'Bhoothalinga Iyer himself signed this. How did this happen?'

'Yes, sir. That is how it was. Rama Iyer made a slight mistake. After all Bhoothalinga Iyer and he are both Brahmins. He wanted to save Bhoothalinga Iyer. It is plain as could be.'

'Then why did you admit all that you have admitted?'

'I have in all honesty admitted nothing.'

'Oho,' shouted Tirumalachar.

'Go on,' said the judge.

'Sir, why do we admit then that a chair is a chair?'

'Why, have you not seen a chair?'

'Ho, ho!' shouted the crowd.

'Has anyone seen a chair?' asked the judge.

'Nobody has,' said the Government Advocate. He was plainly taking sides with the accused.

The judge said: 'I sit on a chair.'

'Who?' asked Govindan Nair.

The judge in fact rose up to see who sat on the chair. He went round and round the table looking at who? There was such silence, the women wept. The cat jumped on to the dais. The attendants said nothing. The Government Advocate was chatting happily with Govindan Nair. Who said there was a case? The clerk was looking for the file to put back the paper. Usha put a garland around the neck of Govindan Nair.

That was the fact. Govindan Nair was not set free. He was free. Nobody is a criminal who has not been proven criminal. The judge had to find himself, and in so doing, he lost his seat. Who sits on the judge's seat became an important subject of discussion in Travancore High Court. Since then many learned treatises have been written on the subject.

It was all due to Govindan Nair. He had, while in prison, written out a whole story to himself. Bhoothalinga Iyer had signed the paper. It had nothing to do with ration permits. It had to do with Bhoothalinga Iyer's extramarital propensities. In this business he came across virtue. So instead of going to Benares he gave the money to the widow of a Brahmin, an Iyengar woman in fact. (The breasts and other things were added to make the story comply with film stories.) The story came true as he wrote it. He was sure that it was a fact. He told himself again and again and told it in court again and again. At night the prison wardens were surprised to see him talking to himself. Actually he thought he was addressing the court. He even made and remade the necessary gestures. Wardens could think he was practising acting. He recited his prose precisely till he knew every situation by heart. That is why he was so cocksure in open court. After all, only a story that you write yourself from nowhere can be perfect. You can do with it what you want to do with it. (Abraham wrote romantic poetry and he said it did with him what it wanted. So, eventually, he married Myriam, etc.) But Govindan Nair had the liberty the judge did not have. Only the Government Advocate knew everything. A fact is a prisoner. You are free, or you become the prisoner, and the fact is free, etc., etc. So the Government Advocate knew the accused was no accused. He was one with the accused. That showed why the cat went to the Government Advocate first. The cat also kissed the clerk on the neck.

Bhoothalinga Iyer's signature was revealed by a sunbeam. Was Bhoothalinga Iyer then in Coimbatore?

Mr Justice Gopala Menon was the son of the late Peshkar Rao Bahadur Parameshwara Menon, and he had only three months of service before retirement. He took leave preparatory to retirement and went to the Himalayas, so people said. Govindan Nair laughed and remarked: 'You no more find the truth in the Himalayas than you find it in the *Indian Law Register*. You may find it on your garden wall and not know it was it. You must have eyes to see,' he said desperately to me.

'What do eyes see?' I asked, as if in fun.

'Light,' he said, tears trickling from his dark eyes.

You only see what you want to see. But you must see what you see. Freedom is only that you see what you see.

Normally the story should have stopped there. But is life normal? Is the cat in the court normal? Are big breasts and a necklace rising and falling at the feet of a ration clerk normal? Is death normal? Is Shantha's life with me normal (she not married to me and such a wife)? And Saroja such a married spouse (and living far away where the Dutch once landed, those able-bodied men), and she keeping Vithal and telling him: 'Your father is no father. Your real father is the sun. Worship him.' And when he falls and rises in prostration every morning, Vithal finds a box of peppermints, round as the

151

sun. This is to prove his paternity. Are the wars normal? Hitler smashing the British in Libya? Are the Japanese normal, those semi-divine, semi-human beings who, never seeing their Emperor, die for him, crash airplanes against British warships, walk through Burmese jungles on famine rations and defeat the bulldog British? And the one plus one that makes two—is that normal, tell me? What then is normal? My new baby is normal. He feeds on his mother's breasts and for the rest he sleeps or cries. Usha looks after him as if it were her own child.

A child for a woman is always her own child. All children belong to her by right. Who made the world thus? I say you made it. Whoever said it was made, made it. Otherwise how can you say it was made? Making itself is an idea born of the world. When making seeks making in making, pray, who sees a world? You say World, and so making comes into existence. Is one the proof of the other? Are you my proof, I ask of you, whoever you may be? Suppose I were to take you to a lonely island and say, coo. The whole island will say coo. Then you say the whole island says coo, forgetting that you said coo. And when you said who said coo, you seek your breath and you know breath said coo. Did you see the origin of your breath? And did you see the origin of your breath? And did you see him who knows you breathe, etc., etc.? It is not so simple as all that. No question is simple. So no answer is normal. Yet must I have stopped where I left off? But I must give you other news. I must prove the world is. For Love is where happening happens as non-happening. What can happen where everything is, etc., etc.?

To prove the world is, I build a house two storeys high. To speak the truth, Shantha's land was sold for eighteen thousand rupees. (The Revenue Board at last gave its decision soon after our child was born.) She paid some of her mother's debts and she and her mother moved to my house completely. We paid the Mudali (who comes every Friday to see Usha and takes her to his wife, from where the child returns rich in gifts of sweets and dolls and many choli-pieces) the second instalment. In regard to the third, we waited for Govindan Nair to come out of jail. He sent word privately that we should not worry. Anyway, the Mudali was so kind to us, a month or two would make no difference to him. Thus with the little money Shantha still had—we started the second storey. Were it only one room and large veranda, it would still do. We just wanted a little more sea air. From the upper terrace we look over the coconut trees (and actually see some eagles' nests), and far away we see the white of the sea. When the Maharaja goes on his Arath procession in the full October evening we will be able to see the elephants and the horses though we could never guess where the sword will be dipped in the sea and the Brahmins will bathe. But when night falls and the procession returns, how beautiful it will look, the clusters of linked lights moving back to the temple, and then all the million million temple lights will be aglow. That is why I said to Usha: 'How can we leave Shantha and the child? We shall see the Arath from here.' Usha said, 'Of course, and Tangamma will come and stand on our terrace.' Modhu, her eldest born, and Govindan Nair will go to the procession. The cat will sit on the edge of the new terrace and see the procession go to the sea.

The cat has become something of a problem to us. It feeds only on white-cows' milk, not even cows' milk will do. Govindan Nair says there are some chemical processes in white cows which are not to be found in black cows, that is why Narayan Pandita Vaidyan always says: 'Take this trituration, sister, and after that you must drink white-cows' milk.' Strange, these limitations man seems to put on himself. However, there it is, the cat appears to understand it better. If Shantha is in her 'three days', and she should by chance touch the white saucer of milk, the cat will not come anywhere near it. If I ever get angry with the cat, it does not get angry with me, but will beg me for milk. Thus it shows what a fool I am. How can you get angry with such a silent thing? Have you ever seen it bite or tear? No, never. Usha can lie by the cat as the baby lies by her, and nothing ever happens, not even a scratch on the nose. Sometimes the cat disappears and one does not see it for a long time. The Mudali, who loves the cat, says it goes on its *swayamavara*[14] rounds. It must seek its mate. But nobody has ever seen our cat meow on our terrace and call for a mate. Then one day it appears on the wall. We never ask it where it has been, it goes back to its white-cows' milk (and the saucer) as if it had never been anywhere. Mysterious are feline ways.

Mysterious, you could say, are man's ways too. He goes shopping or barking as he likes. I say barking because Govindan Nair's shout is so much like a bark sometimes. He must speak to tree and mongoose as if they were under his authority. Everything in the world seems to obey—or must obey—Govindan Nair. I sometimes wonder what would, say, the river Parrar do, if he said: 'Turn this way and go to the Coromandel Sea.' It might become a Coromandel river. He still comes and says many things I just begin to understand. Shantha says in the evening: 'What a strange man. He seems wanting to devour the whole world with fire. Then he sits down and talks

14. An ancient Hindu custom of choosing the bridegroom from an assembly of 'pretenders'.

156

to you as if he were sending a child to sleep. Who is he?' Who, indeed, is Govindan Nair? He says he is a Nair and all Nair land has floated down to Antarctica. Perhaps they keep a record there? But here, what do we know? He has bought himself a bicycle, too. He gave us the next seven thousand rupees a few months after he came out of jail. We gave it to the Mudali. He took the whole sum but kept only four thousand. With the other three thousand, he had a gold belt and two diamond earring made for Usha, and a nose ring for Shantha. (Rather, his wife came home with betel leaf and nut, and this was offered with ceremony.) Shantha looks so lovely with her straight nose, her rich black hair and her diamond nose ring.

A third storey was what I wanted to build, so that I could see up to the end of the sea. Govindan Nair laughed and said, 'Mister, can you see the back of your head?' I said no. 'To see the end of the sea is just like saying: I see the end of your nose. Can you see the end of my nose? Have a good look at it. Can you see it there? Just there. Yes, just here. Can you see it?' he asked. I said, 'No, how can I see a point?' 'Then how can you see the sea?' he asked. 'The drop makes the ocean, is an ancient saying.' 'So what shall I see when I build a house three storeys high?' I said. He said: 'The day that it is finished you will die. I have your horoscope. It is all drawn up. Jupiter enters the seventh house, and with moon in the fifth, death is certain.' The cat jumped on to my lap and sat in comfort, her head held high.

The fact was I dreamed of a house three storeys high. Shantha said: 'Why be so ambitious? Why not be satisfied seeing the Arath from our roof, and vaguely perceive the Maharaja dipping the sword into the sea? You can count the tiers of the temple spire, too.'

I was not satisfied. But one day the cat came back with a hollowed belly. We never knew where the litter was. She had hidden them somewhere, for we could see the teats were out. We never heard the kittens. One afternoon, however, on the wall was a series of four (or was it five or six?) kittens. They were all ambling along. She carried each one from one spot to the other, lifted them by the scruff of the neck. They neither meowed nor did they paw the air. One by one she took them down the wall.

That was the first time I went across the wall. I found a garden all rosy and gentle. There were bowers and many sweet-smelling herbs, there were pools and many orchids that smelled from a distance. There were old men with beards as long as their knees, and they talked to no one. Young men were in green turbans and others, children and women, sang or danced to no tune but to the tune of trees. Snakes lived there in plenty, and the mongoose roamed all about the garden. I saw deer, too. The air was so like a mirror you just walked towards yourself. How is it I never knew my neighbouring wall went up and down the road, and up again towards the hospital and came back by the bazaar and down towards the Secretariat and back again, covering such a large area, as if I could never have seen where it began and where it ended. I had also met some of my neighbours. That man there is in charge of the temple jewels. This man has a small watch shop in

Puttenchantai. This is a famous lawyer and that other was once premier. The school children I recognize well, for I meet them with Usha when I sometimes go to fetch her from her school. How is it I never saw the others anywhere, or when I saw them I did not know they were here, across the wall? The fact of the fact is that I was too lazy to know who lived there. Truly to speak, if Govindan Nair had not come (and with the British bubo and Shridhar the two houses almost became one), I should never have gone beyond my *Malayalarajyam* and the Government Secretariat, with *The Hindu* for the evening tea. There would not have been even Shantha (who came to me because she loved the way Govindan Nair and I talked). Truth is such a beautiful thing—a beautiful woman like Shantha loves to hear the truth talked, because it explains her beauty and takes away her responsibility. Lord, how can anyone bear the burden of beauty?

So that day I walked behind the cat. It went down into the kitchen of the White House and left the litter in the corner of the granary room. Then it went up a series of stone steps. Up and up it went, up the staircase. Everybody bowed as if awed. Then I, too, followed it. This time I would not be defeated. I must win, I said. The winning was easy, for I heard a very lovely music. I was breathless. The staircase suddenly turned, and in went the cat. I stood there white as marble. I looked in and saw everything.

I saw nose (not the nose) and eyes seeing eyes, I saw ears curved to make sound visible, and face and limbs rising in perfection of perfection, for form was it. I saw love yet knew not its name but heard it as sound, I saw truth not as fact but as ignition. I could walk into fire and be cool, I could sing and be silent, I could hold myself and yet not be there. I saw feet. They made flowers on stems and the curved hands of children. I smelled a breath that was of nowhere but rising in my nostrils sank back into me, and found death was at my door. I woke up and found death had passed by, telling me I had no business to be there. Then where was I? Death said it had died. I had killed death. When you see death as death, you kill it. When you say, I am so and so, and you say, I am such and

161

such, you have killed yourself. I remain ever, having killed myself.

This was what Govindan Nair meant. This is what Usha meant when she said she *saw* Shridhar. She did not really, but when she went up, she saw herself and called herself Shridhar. Now I understand. This is also why Govindan Nair never went to prison. When you see the stone of the wall, and stone alone remains, you have no prison. If I say you are and just see you, you are not *there*. If I go on seeing a point, I become the point. So the prison vanished. And I understood the ration-shop scale where children played. You weigh only that which you seem to weigh, but that which knows neither balance nor weight stands outside of time. Life is so precious. I ask you why does not one play?

I play now building my house of two storeys. I change the beams of black wood to those of teak (people say like this white ants don't worm them out). I have a flush lavatory on the other floor so that Usha need not come down during the night. Doctors say the evacuating habits of children form their character later. Besides, Shantha and I love

162

each other so much, sometimes she wants to wash because she wants to love even more. How I love the smell of Shantha's body, it's like the inner curve of a jackfruit—pouch and honey of wondrous odours, and succulent. Oh, how beautiful the earth is.

The cat's litter is at my door. Now that Govindan Nair is transferred to Alwaye, I have my responsibilities. I go on feeding kittens. I gave one of them to Bhoothalinga Iyer's widow the other day. John was gone off to the wars; soon after the knife incident he joined the navy. The battle of Burma was just beginning. His wife, however, came and said: 'Sir, I hear you have a cat that has wonderful kittens. Could you give me one? My husband was a friend of Govindan Nair.' I gave her a cup of tea, some cakes, and one white kitten went with her. (Mrs John was called Anita.) The Iyengar lady with big breasts and all that—she also comes. She plays with the cat (and with Usha when she is free) and goes away. She says her house is too small and she has no place for a cat yet. If Govindan Nair were here, he would find her a house. In the Brahmin streets near the temple there are such lovely dilapidated structures. You can buy any one of them and build it anew. It will fetch pure gold after the war. Sir C.P.[15] will go and Gandhi-raj will come. In Gandhi-raj everybody will have a house.

I will never build a house three storeys high. Have you ever seen a house so high? No, not in Trivandrum. In Trivandrum, the best houses, those of P. Govardhan Nair or of Jagadish Iyer, retired High Court judge, or even of Raja Raja Rajendra Varma, His Highness's first cousin, are but two storeys high. You can make nice curved stairways. You could make one in marble, or in polished wood (like in the Royal Guest House at Kanyakumari), but you must always have the terrace open. That is what one calls the third floor. A house always opens into openness. Has anybody seen a house shut out?

I have been made Secretary of the Temple Grants Department at the Revenue Board. From five Secretaries they increased to eight, because of the serious strain of war work. I

---

15. Sir C.P. Ramaswamy Iyer, the then Dewan of Travancore.

never see my son Vithal—his mother keeps him away so that her lands will not become mine. Shantha never grumbles and says, I want to marry you. How could one not be married in marriage when you move where there is no movement, you sleep where there is but light? Marriage is not a fact, it is a state. You marry because you see.